Because of Ryan

Because of Ryan

Cygnet Brown

Author

Ozark Grannies' Secrets

1

Would he be at the funeral today?

She had not seen him in almost eight years.

The funeral procession with the hearse carrying Harrison Fisher's body snaked its way through the Park Grove Cemetery on the waning August afternoon that Labor Day weekend. The day was an overcast Friday afternoon at the end of the workday.

It was just like Harrison to require the employees to use their time off to attend his funeral, Madison Baton thought.

Dressed in black, Madison unfolded her long legs out from the backseat of the Davidson's olive-green Forester and placed her feet on the ground outside of the car. She lifted her slim body from a sitting position in the car and ducked around the doorframe to stand up. Janice Davidson's husband Roger had driven the three of them to the graveside. Madison had left her old Accord back at the factory, where she would collect it after the graveside service.

"The grave is over this way," Roger motioned his wife and Madison toward the hole in the ground that was surrounded by flowers. A lift stood over the burial site.

"It's hard to believe how suddenly it happened," Madison heard one of her other co-workers say. "One day he's bossing us around and the next he was dead."

The day before the night when he died, Harrison Fisher had been in the office and standing on the catwalk scowling and watching the production staff work. He had died at home while eating alone.

When his employees did not see him come in to work the next morning when he had always been to work before the first warning bell rang, Beca, the receptionist, called his house but got no answer. She left it at that because the employees didn't have time to worry about his whereabouts. He would expect them to make production whether he was there or not. The employees didn't think about their boss until the lunch break bell rang and they filed into the employee lunchroom.

There they learned that their boss's body had been found by the housekeeper. That had occurred on Tuesday. Now, at the cemetery, his employees were part of the crowd gathered around the single open grave.

The crowd, most dressed in black, came to stand around the rectangle dug into the ground. Six men, one whom Madison knew was Harrison's son, Seth, carried the casket from the back of the hearst to the stand beside the gravesite. He wore a dark navy blue suit rather than a black one.

He was there. She should have known he wouldn't miss his own father's funeral.

Madison smiled as she thought about when she and Seth were in high school, and they argued about a specific navy blue blouse that she had. He had said that it was black while she knew that it was blue. Finally, Seth asked her mother what the color was, and her mother, Diane Baton agreed with Madison that the color was blue, not black. Seth Fisher still didn't know the difference between black and navy blue.

Now the men lowered the ornate casket of the finest quality onto the graveside stand. Harrison couldn't take it all with him, but he seemed to try to take as much of it with him as possible. His casket was made of the finest quality wood. Janice, who had been to the viewing said that the Inside was lined with the finest pure white silk. At the viewing, which Madison did not attend, others told her that his hands were folded across his chest. In full display, he was wearing a banded ornately designed but masculine ring. The ring was a white gold ring with a diamond-studded deer antler and rose gold inlay proudly displayed on his left-hand ring finger.

Several people opened their umbrellas, not only because it might rain, but also because the hot sun could come out again at any minute. One of the umbrellas was white and had pictures of Mickey Mouse dancing around it.

Madison shook her head. It was so like old Pete Vails to color outside the lines with his sense of humor. She guessed that at sixty-six Pete had the right to have the gall to use Mickey Mouse to lighten up a funeral.

Madison sat in the back row of the crowd as the crowd including Madison listened to the pastor drone on, sharing glowing lies about the man who had been her boss for the past nearly eight years. The pastor had been paid well to give such a glowing report of Harrison Fisher's life because much of what the minister had to say was a fabrication.

The sound of a lawnmower started up in another part of the cemetery. Several people began to sniffle, not because of the old man's death, but because of the allergies in the air of the pollen from the grass that the lawnmower released hung heavy.

Madison could not think of one of Harrison's employees who was fond of the old man, including herself. Some of her fellow employees said that having his funeral on the weekend was a condition of Harrison Fisher's will. Madison didn't doubt it. Even in death, he seemed only to value his bottom line.

The employees at the funeral had not gone to wish the old man farewell. Mostly they wanted to ensure that he was gone. However, equally important to their curiosity was that they had come to check out what had become of his son Seth, Harrison's son. He had flown in the night before from Germany where he worked at the satellite factory where his mother ran the business as a condition of their divorce.

Seth Fisher then stood to say a few words.

Madison took a deep breath and let it out slowly. Seth was talking, but Madison wasn't listening to what he was saying. She was comparing who he was now with the boy he had been when they were in high school.

Seth looked more mature than when she had last seen him, but then, of course, he did. He was eight years older now. Gone was the boyish charm she remembered. This man was all business. His face was more chiseled, more determined. His wild dark brown hair was tamed with a layered cut that accentuated his handsomeness. He had filled out over the years with a muscular body. and Madison imagined that he must have had washboard abs under that suit. He no doubt worked out at the gym. He had been athletic in high school, and she did not doubt that he still was. It had been his athleticism that was the reason for them getting to know each other in the first place.

"You know he's taking over the business here in Springfield," Janice Davidson, her supervisor, and friend who was standing beside her whispered. "I wonder if he'll be like his father?"

"I have no idea," she whispered back. *She couldn't imagine that he could be like him.* The Seth Fisher that she had known had been nothing like his father, but then, perhaps she never had known him. She wasn't sure what she thought of this stranger in the blue suit. She just wanted to keep her distance and remain invisible. If he did take over the business as the rumors suggested, she would do her best to remain a gray man. She just wanted to do her job and go home every night like she had been doing for eight years.

Before he spoke, Seth Fisher looked out over the crowd.

"It's been a long time since I saw any of you, but I see that there are many familiar faces in the crowd," Seth said. "I do want to thank you all for coming here today to say farewell to my father. It means a lot to me that you are here."

His eyes scanned the crowd and for a moment his eyes seemed to lock onto Madison's eyes. He nodded at her, and she lowered her eyes. She felt a mix of excitement that he still noticed her and the reminder that she had been nothing more than a fling when they were in high school. She didn't want him to discover the secret that she had been hiding for those eight years. She especially didn't want him to know it until she was sure that he was not like his father. She worried that he might have been more like his father than she had thought.

Madison didn't listen to the rest of what Seth had said. She was too busy thinking about how she and Seth had been in the same high school and how they had attended the prom together. She blushed as she remembered that fateful night eight years earlier.

They had dated when they were in high school. Right after graduation, he had gone to college in Europe, and they had lost contact. Now that his father was dead, he had returned to Springfield.

The officiating pastor, Reverend McConnell said a few more words over the casket and Seth placed a wreath of flowers on the casket. No one cried as they watched it lowered into the dark hole.

Madison wondered what everyone was thinking about Harrison's death. She wondered how many who stood here now were relieved that the old man was gone.

Like her, they were also probably wondering how Seth would manage the business as the new CEO. Harrison had made no bones about Seth becoming president of the company when he retired, but instead of retiring, Harrison Fisher had died before Seth had returned. Madison knew that Seth had been groomed to take over the business. After leaving Springfield, he worked for his mother's branch of the company in Germany. He spent the past three years as the Vice President of the German Division of Fisher Spring Industries Incorporated. However, no one had seen him stateside for eight years and now here he was in the flesh.

"Hello, Madison," Seth's voice broke Madison's consciousness.

Madison had been so deep in thought that she hadn't realized that everyone else had moved away from the gravesite and were gathering in little groups near the cars. Nor had she seen that Seth had come to stand beside him.

Janice saw her and waved to her and then nodded. To avoid being rude, Madison smiled up at Seth.

"Hi Seth," she felt like a stupid schoolgirl. She could have kicked herself.

"It's been a long time," Seth replied.

"Yes, it has. I heard you had gotten married."

"That's right. I married several years ago and we divorced almost immediately. It just wasn't right for either of us," he replied.

"I see," she said. She had read about the divorce as well.

"Will you be going to the wake?" Seth asked.

"Ah, no," Madison said. "Janice and Roger Davidson will be taking me back to get my car right after this. Mom will have dinner waiting for me."

"Well, you could come with me, and I'll take you home afterward," Seth replied.

"Ah, no, that's okay. Like I said, Mom is expecting me for supper. I'll see you at work on Monday. I'm sure."

Madison could have kicked herself for admitting that. She didn't want to give him so much personal information.

Seth frowned. "You work at Dad's factory?"

"Yes, I do." *So much for Seth not being aware of her working at the factory. Perhaps he wasn't interested. However, if he wasn't interested, then why did he make a point of approaching her here?*

"Dad didn't tell me that."

"*I am sure he didn't.* she thought. *He had good reasons not to tell Seth anything about her.*

At that moment Janice motioned for her that they were ready to leave.

"I have to go," Madison replied. "My ride awaits."

"I'll see you on Tuesday, then," Seth called back. "Monday is Labor Day."

"Of course," Madison had been so nervous that she had forgotten that Monday was a holiday.

Madison waved a backward hand to him as she hurried away. She felt her whole body shaking over their meeting.

What he would think if he knew that he was the father of Ryan, her son?

2

Madison had lived all her life in the house on Elm Avenue. The Baton house, located on a corner lot at the corner of Elm and Third Street was a white three-bedroom Cape Cod with double dormers and green shutters. The property was located on a corner lot on a quiet street in the town.

The main yard rose above the sidewalk which every couple of Saturdays during the growing season, Madison had to weed-eat rather than mow. Around the level area above the sidewalk were the quintessential white picket fence and front porch with a porch swing. Here Madison lived with her son and her mother Diana. Her father Luther had died when Ryan was three years old.

When they were in high school, Madison used to like to sit with Seth on the porch when she used to do homework. Since he left, she had tried not to think much about him, However, every time she looked at Ryan, she saw the face of his father. Now that he was back in town, she couldn't get Seth off her mind.

Madison's mother Diana was setting the table as Madison entered the front door. The smell of meatloaf and scalloped potatoes rose from the oven. A pan of freshly baked yeast rolls added their aroma to the delicious smells in the room. The cake Diane Baton had baked the day before was in a plastic-covered tin and had three pieces taken from it from the previous night's meal.

"How was the funeral?" Diane set the silverware on either side of the plate at Madison's place at the table.

"Well, you can guess. it was a funeral." Madison opened the oven door and looked at the two dishes on the oven rack. Of course, they were almost done. Her mom was the best cook she knew, and she had a knack for having everything ready for the table at the same time.

"Were a lot of people there?" Diane laid a fork on one side of Madison's plate and a knife and spoon on the other side. She moved on toward Ryan's plate.

Hmm, yeah, mostly people from work." Madison answered. She took a deep whiff of the homemade rolls. "These look yummy, Mom."

Madison took one of the rolls from the basket that they were in and broke it in half.

"Hey, those are for dinner," Diane said.

Well, trust me, it won't ruin my appetite. I'm starved."

"Well, did you talk to Seth?" Diane looked up from her task at hand.

"A little."

"And?" Madison's mother raised her eyebrows. Madison used a similar eye-raising whenever Ryan did something questionable.

"It was just small talk, Mom."

"Did you tell him about. . ." she motioned toward Ryan's place at the table.

"Of course, I didn't! You don't break that kind of news at a funeral, especially his own father's funeral. I wouldn't want him to think that I'm a gold digger or something."

"Well, you'll have to tell him someday. He has a right to know."

"I'll worry about that on Monday.

"You mean on Tuesday. Monday is a holiday."

"Right, Seth reminded me of that too. I don't want to think about that right now, I just want to enjoy the rest of this weekend."

"What if he stops by this weekend?"

"You know he won't stop by this weekend. Our relationship is long over. He moved on a long time ago." Madison went to the cupboard and took out glasses from the cupboard. She looked out the window at the back of the kitchen and saw an empty swing set.

"He may have moved on, but have you?" Diane asked.

"Of course."

"Then why haven't you started dating again."

"You know that I have been out on a few dates," Madison retorted.

"You haven't dated anyone more than a one-nighter since Seth."

"What can I say? I'm picky," Madison slathered butter on the dinner roll. "By the way, where's Ryan?]

"Ryan is at John Carpenter's house. Mandy said that she would bring him home. They should be arriving at any moment now."

As if on cue, the Carpenter's white SUV pulled up in front of the house. The backseat door opened, and seven-year-old Ryan came running up the front stairs.

"Mom!" He exclaimed and threw himself into her arms.

"How was your day, little buddy."

"It was great, Mom. Kitty Rogers threw up all over the cafeteria floor and the janitor had to clean it up with kitty litter. After that, we played soccer in PE class.

"That sounds like fun," Madison exclaimed. She looked down at her son. He had his father's dark brown eyes and dark chestnut-colored hair. He already seemed to have a knack for winning Madison's heart just like his father had when he was growing up. He looked so much like Seth. "Did you have fun at John's house?

"Yeah, he and I played tennis on his Wii, and I beat him!"

"Way to go," Madison gave him a high five. "I'm not surprised. "You're good at sports," He was very competitive and liked winning. Even though he had never met Seth, Ryan was like him in that way too.

She remembered how her father would play with Ryan as a baby and said that he looked like her. Madison knew better. Even as a baby Ryan had looked like Seth. She remembered crying over baby Ryan knowing how much she missed the child's father. She thought those days were over, but those feelings came rushing back. Tears blurred her vision.

Stop it, she told herself silently.

Now Ryan was seven years old, and he looked more and more like his father with each passing day. For a long time, she would cry over him while the boy slept as she mourned her broken heart. The tears had dried up and so had her feelings for Seth. At least that was what she always tried to tell herself. Today, after seeing him, she had to remind herself of that to keep her resolve.

For a long time, Madison had dreamed that Seth would return from Europe and come to tell her that he couldn't live without her. She imagined him taking a taxi up to the sidewalk in front of Madison's house. He would run up the steps and knock on the front door and tell her that he had made a mistake and that he wanted nothing more than to pick up where they had left off.

Those hopes were dashed when she learned that he had married a woman in Europe. Some woman named Bianca Volts. Madison had tried to date for a while but the few men she dated seemed to lack the characteristics that she had always found interesting about Seth. She would go out once, but she never seemed to find that special spark with anyone else. Now she no longer bothered dating. She had Seth's son to raise.

She had thought that perhaps one day, she would get over her first love. Now that she had seen him and talked to him, she had her doubts about that was even possible. Madison stopped crying over the past and was trying to move on with her life. However, Seth's return was already putting a kink in her plans because he was not only Ryan's father, but he was also her boss.

Madison determined that she would not dwell on a possible love life and decided to focus on her life plans. Instead of looking for another relationship, Madison had gone back to school. When Ryan was three, she started taking business classes to move on from the factory into an office job somewhere. Because she had to work full-time to support her son, she was only able to take one class at a time. She hoped to have her bachelor's degree by the time she reached thirty.

Fortunately, her mother had taken over a lot of the responsibility of Ryan so Madison could pursue her career goals. Madison had convinced herself that she did not have time for a social life. She was a mother, a student, and a wage earner. She didn't have time to hunt for a man.

She hoped to get a master's in business someday, but after three years she was still working on her second year of college. She wondered if she would ever be able to finish her degree. Since her father had died, she had to work overtime whenever possible to share the expenses. Even if Diane wanted to pay all the bills, the older woman's social security wouldn't have been enough to cover them. Not that Madison minded taking care of many of the responsibilities. Madison felt that her mother's help with Ryan more than balanced out Madison's help with the household bills.

3

⌘

On Tuesday morning, Madison parked in her usual parking space at Fisher Spring Industries Corporation and made her way past the front offices into the manufacturing part of the building.

On Labor Day, Madison had taken her mother and son to the beach for one last swim before autumn weather settled in for the season. Madison loved watching Ryan playing in the waves. She joined him in the water and the two of them threw a beach ball back and forth. Diane watched from the shore. She didn't enter the water except for her feet. After their swim, the three of them built a fire and cooked hot dogs and smores over an open fire before heading home to prepare for Tuesday and the beginning of the school and work week.

Ryan always liked days like this when they were able to get out. Fortunately, this trip to the beach was inexpensive. Ryan loved these outings and Madison hoped that he would continue to enjoy these kinds of outings as he grew older.

Who was she trying to fool? Eventually, Ryan would want more than she could ever afford to offer him. He needed a male figure in his life like she had needed one in her own life.

Keeping a child costs money. A lot more money than she was making on her salary. She knew that if she wanted to do that, she would have to get her degree, but once she got her degree. she would also have to start paying for her student loans. She had tried to pay for as much of her education as she went along as much as possible, but she still found that she needed to take out loans if she wanted to make ends meet. She wondered

12

how she would pay for everything when Ryan started participating in organized sports. The uniforms, equipment, and fees were not cheap, and she wondered how she would be able to afford the extra expense.

Janice met her in the breakroom at the time clock even before she clocked in. Madison punched in and turned toward her manager and friend.

"Good morning, Madison," Janice asked as she handed her the clipboard for the items that they needed to produce that week. "How was your weekend."

Madison shrugged. "Oh, we went to the beach. How about you?"

"We had a cookout with the kids and grandkids," Janice and Ralph were the same age as Madison's mother. They had four kids and all of them were out of the house. The youngest was a sophomore in college. Their eldest daughter had two kids—a boy and a girl.

"Nice," Madison replied as she looked over the schedule. "Do you know if the iron came in for the XM project?"

"I haven't asked Pete yet, but on Friday morning he said he thought it might be here later this afternoon."

"I hope so," Madison replied. "Machine number 10 will be needed to make many of the parts, and I don't know how well it will behave."

"Yes, but that delay should allow Rhonda Macon to complete the order for Epi-zone Audio."

"Rhonda's on the machine this week?" Madison asked.

Janice nodded, and Madison rolled her eyes. Rhonda liked to gossip more than she liked to work. Madison would have to stay on Rhonda's case if she wanted Rhonda to make her quota this week.

Madison knew she had a way with people to get them to do what she wanted, no, make that, she needed them to do. She was kind, but thorough, Janice wrote on her most recent personnel review. She had said that Madison got along with everyone in the plant, especially her manager.

They respected one another and that was important in a small town like this one.

Madison had been a loyal worker for eight years at the factory and a few months ago, she had become Janice's assistant manager of her portion of the production floor. At first, Harrison Fisher had personally objected to the promotion, but Janice insisted that Madison be moved up to assistant floor manager. Though Madison had worked at the plant longer than Janice or her husband Ralph, many people came to her with questions rather than to Janice. Harrison finally agreed to allow Madison to take the job temporarily and he put her on probation in the management position. Because it was only a temporary position, he was not paid for the extra work that she was doing.

Rather than seeing Madison as a threat to her position Janice had taken the younger woman under her wing. For this Madison was grateful. Even though no one faulted Madison for her ability to do the job, Harrison had not given the job to Madison permanently, and she was still on probationary status.

Janice had confided with Madison that she didn't understand why Harrison Fisher had overlooked the younger woman for advancement, but Madison knew the reasons that she had not been given many of the promotions that she had applied for over the years. It wasn't because she had not been qualified. She had worked in every position on the floor at least once and knew every nook and cranny of the place. She probably knew the day-to-day operations of the plant better than many of the other employees in management did including Harrison. The problem that kept Madison from advancing was that Harrison Fisher resented the fact that she was the mother of his only grandson.

Cat Marshall, one of the machine operators, came up and stood beside Madison.

Cat was a beautiful blonde with blue eyes and a perfect body. She had been a freshman in high school when Madison was a senior. She had only been working at the factory for six months.

"Hi, Madison, I was wondering if you could help me with my machine."

"Did it break down again?" Madison asked.

"Yes, you know how it is. The machine knew that it was a holiday weekend and decided to take another day off," she replied. This was a different machine than the one that Rhonda was running, but this one too often had problems. Several of the employees who had worked in other factories had said that the machines here were archaic and should be replaced. Madison wasn't surprised because Harrison Fisher never wanted to spend more money than he had to, which was one of the reasons that he kept Madison on probationary status. He kept her on probationary status so he wouldn't have to start giving her raises quite so soon. The pay scale didn't come into effect until the employee was permanently in that position.

"Can't you get one of the mechanics to help you?" Madison asked. She had been told to always ask that question before taking matters into her own hands.

"No, they're both resetting up a couple of machines. One is working on Rhonda's machine and won't be able to help me within the next hour."

"And the other?" Madison asked.

Cat shrugged. "I don't know. I haven't been paying attention to him."

Madison had operated the machine herself and knew what to do. She had dealt with this machine practically since the day she started working at the factory. The machine should have been replaced years earlier, but Harrison had little interest in upgrading his equipment any more than he wanted to give employees wage increases.

Madison grabbed a wrench from the box beside the machine. She tagged out the machine and crawled under it and began tearing it down to get to the problem. While she worked on the machine, she got oil on her clothes and face. That happened every time she worked on that machine. Just as she finished fixing the machine, Cat sat down at the machine and gave her a thumbs up.

Cat looked past Madison. She gasped. "There's our handsome boss. Oh, my gosh he's coming this way!"

Cat started running her hand over her hair. Madison removed the tag from the breaker and started to stand up.

"How often does that happen?" she heard a familiar male voice behind her. Her heart leaped in her chest. Cat had not been joking when she said the boss was coming.

Cat spoke before Madison had a chance.

"About every week or so," Cat said. "It's good that Madison knows what she does about every machine in the company. It's a wonder she's not one of the grease monkeys."

Madison wasn't fond of being compared to a "grease monkey", but she would let it go. She was more conscious of Seth standing in front of her, and she was covered with machine grease.

"Does she now?" he asked. He then turned toward Madison. He looked at her face and then pulled a tissue from his pocket. "You have. . ."

He pointed at her face and handed her the tissue. She felt herself turn red as she took the tissue and rubbed it on her face.

A little more to the left," he said pointing to a spot on his face. "Good, you got it. Now, could you come with me to my office, Madison?"

"Yes, sir," she said. A quick expression crossed his face that made her realize that he did not like the idea that she called him 'sir'.

She followed him past the breakroom door and through the door that led to the office area. There on the left side of the hall was the office that had been Seth's father's office.

Seth motioned for Madison to have a seat across from what had been his father's desk. Rather than sitting in the chair behind the desk, Seth moved the chair to her side of the desk and sat face-to-face with her.

"I just spent the past few minutes watching you from upstairs, Madison."

Madison felt her stomach somersault. Was he getting ready to fire her?

She was not aware that Seth had been watching her from upstairs. Above the factory floor was a catwalk that was windowed in. Harrison had often watched his workers from that vantage point and Seth was taking up the same habit.

"I'm sorry, but I was told that I was able to work on the machines if the mechanics weren't available."

"Don't apologize. You have nothing to worry about. I find your resourcefulness admirable," Seth replied. "I applaud anyone whose goal is to keep production going. There's nothing worse than a bottleneck in production. I didn't call you here to reprimand you. I asked you here to offer you a proposition.

"What kind of proposition?" Madison asked.

Seth laughed. "Trust me, it's nothing illicit. "I want you to become my personal assistant."

"Why me?"

Because I think you're the right person for the job," Seth replied. "You come highly recommended.

"Who?"

"That's not important. You just come highly recommended. Just say yes."

"Considering our past, do you think that's wise? I mean it would be believed that it was favoritism."

"This has nothing to do with our past, Madison. That was a long time ago. This is business. Not only did I watch you this morning, but I also read what Janice wrote about you in your personnel records. You have quite an impressive record, and I need someone like you who knows the job. I didn't definitively decide you were that person until I watched how you handled your fellow employee and that machine. It convinced me that what Janice said was true, you know this business, at least the production side of this business, and I need you to teach me what you know so I can better serve the employees."

"I see." Madison was deep in thought. She wasn't sure that she wanted to work that closely with Seth, but she knew that the opportunity was something she shouldn't pass up.

"Your personnel record says that you have been working on your business degree." Seth continued.

"Yes, but I haven't yet completed two years."

"I didn't see that you put in any paperwork to get tuition reimbursement from the company. Why haven't you applied for it yet?"

"I didn't know that it was available," Madison replied.

"Is that so?" Seth asked and wrote something down on a piece of paper. "We're going to take care of that right away. Your business degree would be an asset to the business."

'Why, thank you," Madison said.

"Once I get up to speed with the business here, we'll do something about that. In the meantime, you can do on-the-job training as well as go to classes."

"What makes you think that I can go from laborer to administration?"

Seth smiled and leaned his head back. He closed his eyes. "Well, I seem to remember that you were always good at figuring things out."

"That doesn't make me administrative material though. What if I'm not ready for this?"

"This is just business. Based on what I remember about you and from the glowing reports that Janice wrote about you, I believe that you can do this. However, if I am wrong, you can always go back to the floor and your old position as assistant manager no further probation would be necessary either. Does that sound like a deal?"

"I don't know," Madison replied.

"If you want, I'll give you a day or two to think about it."

Suddenly, Madison thought about what her accepting the position and having the company pay her tuition would do not only for herself and her family but also what it would do for the other employees at the plant if she took this position. There would be someone in the administration who would stand up for them for a change. Someone who had been where they were now, someone like her.

"I don't need a day or two. I know what my answer is. I accept your offer," Madison replied.

"Great!" Seth exclaimed. He stood up and put out his hand. "It's a deal. I see no reason you can't start tomorrow."

"It's a deal!" Madison also stood up and put her hand into his firm grip. Her heart fluttered.

She reminded herself. *This is just business. This is just business.*

4

After work, but before going home that evening, Madison attended her business class. Her class was about managing business processes. Because she would now be working as the assistant to the CEO of the business, she had more incentive to know more about how the business worked.

The teacher stood before the class. "This week, we'll be dealing with the OSHA laws. Who knows what OSHA is?"

Madison had read the material over the weekend and now was taking copious notes. She was determined to understand and implement the laws so that the company didn't face any surprises from that government agency in the future. She didn't know how well Harrison Fisher followed the laws, but as she listened to the lecture, she realized that she knew that the company was rife with violations, She also knew that because Seth had spent the last few years in Europe, he may not have been as knowledgeable about OSHA laws either This could be one of the areas where she could make a difference for the company by ensuring that they followed the laws She decided to look more into these laws. Not only would it be good for her to take a deep dive into OSHA for the business, but the knowledge would also help her get a good grade in the class.

A win, win, she thought.

After class, Madison arrived home. Ryan was sitting at the table finishing up his dinner.

"Mommy!" he exclaimed and ran to Madison.

"How are you doing buddy?" she asked.

"Great, Mom!"

"I'm glad to hear it. Did you get your room cleaned yet?"

Ryan had made a mess of his room over the extended weekend, and it was still a mess that morning.

"Ah, Mom!" Ryan did his famous pout that at one time she thought that face he made was cute, but recently realized it was just Ryan's way of manipulating her.

Madison refused to give in to his manipulation. "Put your plate in the sink and go ahead and clean your room. Right now, I'm eating dinner, and then I will be helping Grandma wash dishes. When I'm done, I'll come up to see how much of your room you've cleaned. If you get it done, maybe tomorrow night we can do something special. Matter of fact, if you get it done by the time, I finish helping Grandma with dishes, I will let you watch your favorite cartoon tonight before going to bed."

"Alright," Ryan said begrudgingly and went up the stairs.

Madison took her plate from the table and helped herself to the dinner salad. She then applied a generous slathering of Catalina dressing on the greens.

Madison's mother rinsed Ryan's plate and silverware and put that place setting into the dishwasher.

'So how was your day?" she asked as she placed her place setting into the dishwasher.

Madison smiled a sly smile.

"Seth Fisher promoted me to be his personal assistant," She took a bite of her salad and watched her mother's reaction.

Diane Baton's lower jaw dropped. "Are you serious?"

Madison swallowed her bite of food. "Uh-huh. I wouldn't lie about a thing like that. I start tomorrow."

"Oh, really. And you told him about Ryan? Right?"

"Of course not, I wouldn't have taken the job if the reason he was giving me the job was because he knew that I gave birth to his son. I don't accept charity."

"It wouldn't be charity. You've worked hard for that promotion, and you know it," Diane said.

"But I don't want anyone to think that I was offered the job because I told him about Ryan. I don't that anyone would believe that he had given me the promotion for the same reason that his father gave me a job. To keep me from trying to extort money from them."

"I think you're not being fair to Seth," her mother replied. "He has a right to know that he's Ryan's father."

"Well, I don't know why I must tell him anything. Why should I? He left here without even telling me goodbye."

"You know as well as I do that was more Harrison Fisher's doing than it was Seth Fisher's," Madison's mother said. She took a plate from the stack by the pot on the stove and handed it to Madison. "Spaghetti?"

"Yes, please," Madison piled some spaghetti and sauce with meatballs onto her plate and took her piece of garlic bread from the oven tray.

"Well, you know that Seth is not like his father, don't you? Harrison wanted nothing more than to separate the two of you. I don't believe Seth has those motives."

"But Seth didn't try to get in touch with me the whole eight years."

"Be fair, Madison! Seth was just a boy when he left here."

"And I was just a scared, pregnant girl," Madison replied. "Besides, I'm guessing that I wasn't good enough for him. When he left, he obviously didn't give me another thought. He certainly found someone else soon enough. He got married. Remember?"

"And if you remember, his marriage to that Bianca girl didn't last long either, Madison. You've done nothing to be ashamed of or afraid of. You don't have to be afraid that he's going to take Ryan away from you."

"I'm not afraid of that!" Madison exclaimed.

"Good. Madison, you know that I know you better than that. Just remember, you have nothing to worry about. You have done a good job raising your son," her mother said.

"That's not what I'm afraid of," Madison said. "I don't want Ryan to get hurt if Seth. . ."

"You're afraid that Seth will desert him like he did you. Don't you? I am sure that Seth will regret not being able to have a relationship with his son before now. I'm sure he will be a good father. You must tell him."

Madison didn't want to tell Seth Fisher anything about Ryan. Yes, she was afraid. Ryan's family was one of the richest families in the area and crossing any of them could mean trouble.

She now believed that her infatuation with Seth had blinded her to who he was. He had a crush on Seth much sooner than he even knew she existed. From her freshman year in high school through her junior year, Madison had admired Seth from a distance. He was one of the popular kids and she was not. He had been the captain of the football, basketball, and baseball teams. He was the star of those teams and for girls, the mark of popularity in their school was to have a date with Seth Fisher. Madison never figured she had a chance even to get a token dance from Seth, but in the summer before their senior year, all that changed.

Whereas Seth had been a jock, Madison had been a nerd. Every year she was top of her class academically with a 4.0 average, and she was destined to be the class valedictorian. However, at the end of her junior year, her position in the high school social hierarchy was about to change.

One bright summer morning, between their junior and senior years, Madison's parents got a call from the school principal.

"You want us to what?" Madison's father asked. "Well, I think she would. She's been looking for a way to make money this summer. What would it entail?"

"Okay, I'll bring her into your office. When would be a good time?" he asked into the phone. "Okay, we'll be there."

"What is it, Max," Diane asked.

"Mr. Hunter wants Madison to come in and see about tutoring one of her fellow students," Max Baton replied.

"Who is the student?" Madison asked. "You said something about money. Did he say how much the student was willing to pay?

"He didn't say, he just wants us to meet him in his office this afternoon at one."

Though Madison could have driven her parent's car to the school, Madison's father and mother decided to accompany her to the principal's office.

When they arrived, outside the office, they saw Seth sitting in one of the chairs outside the principal's office. He was flipping through a sports magazine and didn't look up at the three as they came to the door.

Before they had a chance to knock at the principal's door, Principal Hunter opened the door to his office. Come right in.

Inside the office, Harrison was sitting with the principal.

Madison's heart skipped a beat. *Could Seth be the student she was supposed to tutor?*

Harrison Fisher did not stand when they entered the room. He had one leg crossed over the other and his hands were folded in his lap.

Principal Hunter motioned for Madison and her parents to have a seat and he sat in his chair on his side of the desk.

Principal Hunter spoke. "Let's get right to the issue at hand. Mr. Fisher here is looking for a tutor for his son, and I can think of no one better suited for teaching young Mr. Fisher than your daughter Madison."

"I personally would have preferred another young man, but Mr. Hunter here is convinced that your daughter is perfect for the job." Harrison had a superior droll when he talked to anyone who was a person he didn't consider part of his social class.

"We are proud of our daughter," Madison's father said. "She's a hard worker."

Now all these years later, Madison missed her father. He had been what you would expect of a college professor. He had a balding head and a graying goatee. He made it a point throughout Madison's life that she should use her brain rather than her body to get what she wanted from life. Madison's love of books was a common family trait. Both of her parents read books regularly.

"As I am with Seth. However, unlike your daughter, lately because of so much concentration on sports, his grades have been slipping which is why we are looking for someone to tutor him. She can do it, can't she?"

Madison had an instant dislike for Harrison Fisher. He was talking as though Madison wasn't there, and she didn't like being treated like a commodity.

"What do you think, Madison? Max Baton said. "Would you like to tutor Seth Fisher?"

"There would be a sizable salary for your time," Harrison said and named a price.

The fact that there would be considerable money at stake and that she would be spending time with Seth Fisher piqued Madison's interest. It didn't matter that she wasn't fond of his father. "How much time would it require?"

"I was thinking a couple of hours every night ought to be enough time," Harrison replied.

"That would mean that you'd have to forego chess club and math quiz this summer," Madison's mother reminded her.

"That's okay. I'll do it," Madison replied. She knew that her parents were struggling financially. Her father's job paid the bills, but just. Her mother was a homemaker and even though she would have liked to have had a job, she felt that it was best for Madison if she stayed home until the girl was in college. The extra money would help pay for some of Madison's wants in her last year in high school as well as help put a little in the bank toward her college tuition.

"If you're sure," Madison's father said.

Madison looked at her father. She saw that he was concerned about Harrison Fisher's holier-than-thou attitude toward people of their economic stature.

"I am," Madison replied. She would be spending time with the most popular boy in school. Of course, she couldn't pass that up.

Once Madison determined that she was going to tutor Seth, they all went back into the hall where Seth was still sitting and flipping through one of the magazines in the magazine rack.

"Well, I got a tutor for you," Harrison said to Seth.

Seth stood up. "Yes, sir?"

"Yes, I have hired Madison Baton here."

"Madison, weren't you in Mr. Black's Geometry class last year?"

"That's right. You were in the same class."

"You were smart. I wish I had studied with you last year. It would have made this year a lot easier."

Madison smiled. "Maybe."

Seth smiled back and that gave her goosebumps.

Seth may not have seemed to have noticed her as a girl, but he at least had noticed her academic abilities. That was at least something.

"If I remember right, you're good in math, yourself," she replied.

"Thanks," he shrugged and gave a nonchalant half-smile.

At the same time, Harrison butted in. "Well, if you're so good at math, then why did you get a B minus on your last report card?"

Seth just ignored his father. "I look forward to working with you, Madison."

At first, Madison thought that because Seth always seemed so easy-going he would not take his studies seriously, but that was not the case. Because Madison took her tutoring seriously, Seth took her help seriously too.

Over the summer, Madison worked with Seth and helped him improve his math score during summer school. By the time football season started, his overall grade average was up to Harrison Fisher's standard for his son. As a result, Madison's bank account grew and so did Seth's admiration of Madison.

"They say that you will probably be this year's MVP in football," Madison said the night before football practice started.

"Yeah, well, we'll see. I don't know that I'm that good." Seth said quietly.

"Have you ever thought about being a professional player? I'm sure you could get a football scholarship for any college in the country."

Seth shook his head. "I just play because I love the game. If I were going to be a professional player, I might consider that, but being a professional player has never been my goal or my father's goal for me. I just play because I like playing. I would hate to make it a full-time job."

"So why does your father let you play sports?" Madison asked. "I mean. He doesn't seem like the kind of person who would indulge in fun."

Seth laughed. "Yeah, you've got Dad figured out. He indulges my desire to participate in sports because he read somewhere that sports enforce leadership abilities by promoting teamwork and discipline. He expects me to take over his business someday."

"I guess that makes sense. That still doesn't explain why he feels you must go to Europe for your education."

That's because, since their divorce, my mother has managed our business in Germany. Dad is raising me in the United States, with the agreement that I live in Europe with Mom when I'm in college."

"So, your mother runs a branch of the spring business in Germany?"

'Yeah, Dad's letting me see how they do things in Germany, you know because they are so engaged in engineering and all in that country. He thinks that going there will help give me an edge when it comes to our business. He believes that I must always stay one step ahead of my competition."

"Which is why you now have me as your tutor. He wanted you to have an edge. Not only will you go in sports, but you will also be educated."

"Yeah, which is why when my sports activities started interfering with my education, I was in trouble. I begged him to let me continue doing sports. That's when Dad asked the principal to find a tutor for me. He said that if he didn't find someone, he would pull me out of the sports programs and discontinue his support of the school. If the tutor the principal offered didn't help me pass my classes with stellar grades, he was going to send me straight to Germany, do not pass go, do not collect two hundred dollars. He was not going to let me miss out on getting into a good school in Germany just because I wanted to play high school sports. He's holding it over my head that if I didn't do well, he would pull me from every sports program. Fortunately, thanks to you, my grades are improving."

Seth's father paid Madison well for the work she did with Seth. Because Seth got a good grade in his summer math class, Harrison paid her well. Seth passed his summer classes with an A and Madison's college savings account grew.

For a few weeks after summer school ended and before school started, Seth went to football camp and then football practice so Madison didn't see him again until the first day of school.

When the school year started, Harrison encouraged Madison to tutor Seth in several courses. Though he didn't need her to tutor him in math, they were in the same calculus class together, and they did their home-work together. However, she did tutor him in German, physics, and English literature. Madison suggested that since he was going to school in Germany it be a good idea for him to take first-year German. She was taking fourth-year German and knew that she could help him excel in that language.

Because she spent so much time with Seth, her social life changed considerably. The fact she had money of her own to spend also helped in that department. She began to purchase more stylish clothes and used better quality makeup. One day in October, she came into the school without her glasses.

"Contacts?" Seth asked.

Madison nodded.

"You have the most beautiful blue eyes I have ever seen," he smiles. Madison felt her heart pounding. She blushed.

"Thank you."

She liked the idea that Seth noticed her eyes. It was then that she knew that she had fallen for his boyish charm.

When Seth was nominated for King of the Homecoming dance, he nominated Madison. She, of course, didn't win, but she did enjoy a place on the homecoming court, all thanks to Seth.

The football season ended, and basketball season began. Madison let herself forgo participating in the annual play so that she could spend more time with Seth.

Because Harrison Fisher pulled strings, Madison was able to go with the basketball team and attend the away basketball games. During the second semester, Seth seemed to be having an especially difficult time in Geology.

"If you help me get an A in geology, I'll take you to the prom.".

"Really?" By now, Madison was falling in love with Seth. He was her knight in shining armor and the door to popularity that she had been craving up to that point.

He got his geology grade and received an A and all he needed was to pass the final with a good grade which Madison knew he was prepared for.

"So, have you bought your dress for the prom yet? Seth asked.

"I thought you were joking about taking me to the prom," Madison said.

"Of course, I'll take you! What do you take me for? Besides, there's no one I would rather go to the prom with than you."

"Well, I was thinking that since we don't have your final grade yet..."

"Why wouldn't I pass with a good grade? I know the material. Don't you have enough faith in yourself to believe that your student will do well on the test?"

"Of course, you'll do well," Madison said. "You know this information as much as I do."

Seth looked surprised. "Don't tell me that you thought I would renege on my promise to you."

"Well, I," Madison replied.

Now Seth looked hurt. "You didn't think that I was that kind of guy, did you?"

"I..."

"I would never do something so cruel to you, Madison," he said. "You have no idea what you mean to me."

Madison was sure that what he meant was that her tutoring helped him meet his goals.

That weekend, Madison took some of her money out of the bank and decided to treat herself to the best. Her mother helped her choose her dress.

She found a dress she loved. It was a beautiful strapless sweetheart mermaid-style sequined gown in royal blue. The dress brought out the blue in her eyes. The strapless gown accentuated her cleavage. The dress formed around her slim body and accentuated her curves. She felt like a princess.

She left the dressing room to show her mother. "What do you think?"

"Oh, Madison, you look beautiful," she exclaimed.

Madison looked at the price tag. "Oh, Mom, I don't know. This dress was equal to two weeks' pay!"

"I think it's perfect, don't you."

"Oh, I don't know, Mom. It's so expensive."

"You only go to the prom once in a lifetime, Madison. Spend what you need to look your best for one of the most important days of your young life. If you ask me, that dress will make your prom night a magical night."

Madison decided to take her mother's advice and go all out to look her best. On the afternoon of the prom, she went to a nail salon and had her nails done. She had her hair done up in curls and piled on her head. She then had her makeup done professionally. As she looked at herself on the night of the prom, she felt as though her fairy godmother had visited and this was her Cinderella moment. The difference between Madison and Cinderella was that Madison's Prince Charming knew who she was.

Madison would never forget that evening. It truly was magical. Madison was putting the final touches on her outfit when her father announced that Seth had arrived.

Seth's and her father's eyes were on her as she descended the stairs. Her father's eyes shone with pride. Seth's eyes smiled at her, but she saw something else in his eyes too. At the time she didn't recognize it as desire. His jaw had dropped. He was awestruck. This had to have been a magical moment for him too. Her mother had been right. That two weeks' pay had been well spent.

As she stepped from the last step down to the platform at the bottom of the stairs, Seth held out a box containing a wrist corsage.

"Let me put this on you," he smiled. His smile was genuine.

Madison nodded and allowed him to take the corsage from the box and put it on her wrist. His touch was like electricity on her arm. Every fiber of her body quivered as he took her elbow.

"You both have a good time," Luther Baton said to the two of them and said to Seth. "Now you take care of her. You hear me, young man?"

"Yes, sir," he said and led her out the front door and down to his car on the street.

As they settled into his car he said, "I am so lucky to be taking the prettiest girl to the prom."

He leaned over toward her. He lowered his head and ever so gently lowered his lips to hers. The kiss was sweet. Madison felt her stomach do a flip-flop. She felt that Seth must have felt about her that she had about him. She thought that this had to have been the most memorable moment of the night, but it was just the beginning of a new reality.

5

The prom was like a dream. The junior class had turned the gym into a wonderful fairyland with twinkling lights and a live band. Girls dressed in some of the finest dresses that money could buy, and their hair fixed like they were royalty.

Despite the other expensive dresses that the girls wore, Seth and Madison had the attention of everyone in the room. Madison saw several of the girls whispering to other girls and she and Seth passed by. For once, Madison didn't feel anxious about how the other girls were looking at her nor did she feel like a nerd. She knew she had nothing to be ashamed of. She knew that for once she fit into this world or at least she did for this night. The Cinderella analogy came into her mind again.

Seth didn't leave Madison's side all night and she was the envy of every other girl. Dancing in his arms was amazing. It was like a dream and the dry ice effect that was used helped with that effect. She especially enjoyed the slow dances when she could melt into his arms. She didn't want the night to end.

As they danced, Seth whispered in her ear. "Some friends and I have managed to secure a suite of rooms uptown for tonight, and I would like you to come with me."

"Yes," Madison said. She didn't want this Cinderella night to end at midnight. This would be a way for her to keep it going a little longer. She hoped to feel his lips on hers again. There was an after-the-prom party at the local Elks Lodge that was going on all night so Madison's parents wouldn't be looking for her to come home until morning. She wasn't going to tell them she had other plans. What they didn't know wouldn't hurt anyone.

Madison knew that this had to be love. What else could it be? Seth loved her as much as she knew that she loved him. Why else would she be able to feel his love now? She loved having his arms around her as they moved on the floor in a slow dance. She didn't want to think about his going to Germany in a few days and that he would be thousands of miles away. She had to keep her mind on the magic of the evening. Time for missing him would happen later when he was gone. For now, she wanted only to be in his arms. She didn't want this night to end.

They danced until the last song and as they turned on the lights at the end of the night,

"Are you ready?" Seth asked. He kissed her forehead.

Madison nodded and he had his arm around her as they made their way to the car. He opened the car door for her and then closed the door for her once she was settled inside the car. She felt like a princess.

The hotel was not far from the school so within ten minutes they arrived at the room.

"I already have a key to the room. The other guys and I secured the room earlier, so we won't need to stop at the front desk."

"How thoughtful," Madison replied. Seth pulled up in a parking space at the back of the hotel and came around to help Madison out of the car.

"The suite is on the top floor so we will have to take the elevator," Seth said. He led her down a long hallway to where the elevators were and pushed the button. The doors opened immediately. They stepped into the elevator. There Seth took her into his arms and kissed her. Between the elevator movement and that kiss, Madison felt herself swoon.

"You are so beautiful tonight, he whispered into her ear.

The three other members of the basketball team and their dates were already in the hotel suite that they had rented for the night.

The suite was beautiful. It had a spacious living area that had a fireplace in the corner at the far end of the room. Someone had already lit it and it gave a comfortable ambiance to the room. At the end of the room nearest the door was a kitchenette. Above the fireplace, a television hung on the wall. A gray cloth sectional with its back to the door faced the fireplace. Two of the other couples were already making out on the couches.

Madison had expected that they would spend at least part of the night sitting around talking, everyone else seemed to have other ideas. Instead of talking, they were already pairing off. As Seth and Madison stood at the door, another couple came in. They were both laughing and giggling and headed straight for one of the bedrooms and closed the door.

Seth whispered to Madison, "We drew straws, and I drew the other bedroom."

Madison looked over at the other two couples and saw that they were oblivious to Seth and her.

"Okay," she replied.

They went into the bedroom and Seth closed the door to the room. Seth went over to the bathroom and at the sink outside of the shower area, Seth took off his jacket and tie and hung them up. He then took off his shirt. Madison blushed. She had seen him without his shirt on before, but this time she knew that what he had in mind involved her.

"Let's get you a little more comfortable," he said.

She knew instinctively that he expected her to take off her dress.

Madison bit her lower lip. Suddenly she was feeling scared. "I have never…"

If Seth had reacted any other way than he had, she might have turned and run, but he looked at her with compassion. What he said next made her heart feel like it was melting.

Oh, my sweet girl," he said and kissed her. "I'll be as gentle as I can."

He went around to her back and kissed her on the neck and as he did so, he lowered the zipper on the back of her dress. The next thing she knew, her dress was in a puddle at her feet. One by one they removed each other's clothes. Their mouths joined as each item fell. Soon they were both naked. Madison didn't want to think. She just wanted to experience what it would be like for her first time with Seth.

Early the next morning, Madison awoke with a start. At first, she didn't know where she was but then she turned and saw Seth in the bed beside her.

What had they done?

Madison quickly got dressed and Seth took her home. He kissed her at the door. His hand was firmly on her bottom as though to remind her that they were a couple.

"I'll call you later this afternoon," he said as Madison unlocked the front door of her parent's home.

Madison nodded. "Alright.'

The next three weeks after the prom was a whirlwind of activity as all high school seniors are familiar with. There was senior finals week. Both Madison and Seth got straight A's. There was picking up their cap and gowns. Then there was graduation practice and finally graduation. Everyone was smiling and happy to be moving on to college and beyond.

Madison didn't realize that her life was about to take a turn she had not expected.

The morning of Seth's graduation party, Madison was feeling sick. She didn't think much about it. She guessed that it was probably nerves. This was the first time that she had been invited to Seth's house. Seth hadn't hung out at home much himself. He and his father didn't get along well, and his father had often spent much of his time at work so Seth was on his own. He never wanted to meet Madison there. He would always meet her at her house or the library.

When Madison had asked him why they had never met at his house, he told her that he preferred to meet at her house because he liked her parents and liked the peace he felt when he was at her house.

Madison drove her parents' car to Seth's house that day after graduation. Her father had often driven by the Fisher house and Madison was familiar with the rod iron gates near the road flanked by tall brick walls which were covered with ivy. She pulled up to them and stepped out of her car.

"Are you here for young Mr. Fisher's party," a voice called out.

At first, Madison didn't know where the sound was coming from but upon looking toward the sound, she realized that the voice had come out of an intercom.

"Yes, I am," she replied.

"Alright then," Madison got back into the car and watched as the gate opened. She pulled through the gate.

She followed the brick driveway up to the house.

The house was bigger than any she had ever been in. The brick driveway flowed into a circular drive-in front of the house. At the front door, a valet opened the door and allowed Madison to exit the vehicle and then he parked her car for her. Where he parked the car was anyone's guess, but Madison noticed that several valets were speaking to drivers, getting their keys, and driving the car away. So many valets were hired for the event that no one seemed to have to wait. At the door, Madison was ushered into the house by a man dressed in a suit.

Inside, the butler led Madison to the pool area where everyone was milling around the pool, and food and drinks were served.

There Seth met her and handed her a soda.

He then put his arm around her and whispered in her ear. 'How's my little savior?"

Seth handed her a glass of her favorite soft drink and Madison raised her glass. "To Seth! Congratulations on graduating high school with honors!"

"Here! Here!" everyone exclaimed.

Another toast," Seth said, raising his glass of Coca-Cola. "To my little savior who without her, we would not have won our football and basketball trophies! Nor would I likely be getting into that fancy college my father and my mother want me to attend in Germany!"

"To Madison!" The other guests in the room raised their glasses.

They all drank to Madison's health.

It was then that the weight of Seth's leaving struck Madison's heart. Seth was leaving town for a long time. He was leaving. She had been so focused on spending time with him that she hadn't thought about him leaving for good, or at least for a long time. There was no way that she could afford to go to Europe and that was where he was going to school.

How was their relationship going to continue if he was so far away? Suddenly she felt lonely even though he was still standing beside her with his arm around her.

"How soon will you be leaving?" Madison asked.

"Don't worry, Madison. We'll at least have the summers together as well as Christmas vacations."

The day was a dream until Harrison spoke to her at the pool house. Seth had told her to bring her swimsuit because it would be a pool party. He showed her where the pool's shower area was and there Madison changed into the bikini that she had recently purchased as she was leaving the women's area in the tiny room off the pool, Harrison.

"Well, hello, Madison," Harrison said. "You're having a good time, I see."

'Yes."

"Well, it's too bad your time with Seth is coming to an end. You have been a good influence on him. I can see that."

"Thank you, sir, perhaps it doesn't have to be the end," Madison said.

"Oh, I see. Are you stuck on Seth? Well, you can forget about that. Seth will be going to Germany, and I am sure that he will meet other girls."

Madison didn't know how to react, and at that moment Seth came over to where she was standing.

"Come along, Madison, let's go for a swim!"

"Excuse me, sir," Madison felt relieved not to have to continue this conversation with Harrison Fisher.

The following day, Madison got a call from Seth.

"Hi, Madison, well, today's the day," Seth replied.

"Yeah, are you calling for a ride to the airport?"

"No, but I would like to see you before I leave. Can you meet me at the airport?"

"Sure, I would be happy to," Madison replied.

Madison wasn't sure why Seth had not allowed her to take him to the airport but wanted her to meet him there.

Then she wondered if perhaps it was because his father wanted to see him off as well. In the next sentence, Seth verified his

"My father insists on taking me to the airport. I'm sure you understand."

Of course, she understood. Harrison wanted his son all to himself. The fact that Seth wanted her to meet him at the airport meant a lot to her.

Seth told her to meet him at a specific terminal.

"Alright. I'll see you there."

Madison got dressed in a blue sundress that she had recently bought. She carefully touched up her makeup and drove herself to the airport to see him off.

She parked her car in the short-term parking section and started toward the terminal where Seth said he would be. Before she made it to the terminal, Harrison Fisher stepped out in front of her.

"Hello, Mr. Fisher," Madison said.

"What brings you here?" Harrison asked.

"Seth asked me to see him off," Madison replied.

"I think that it would be best for everyone involved if you and Seth didn't see one another anymore."

"Why not?"

"First of all, your work with my son is done," he replied. "He needs to focus on his education and then his career. I don't want you to have any more contact with him."

"You don't have any right to tell me that about him," Madison retorted. "He can associate with anyone he wants. He's a legal adult now."

"It doesn't matter because I am paying his bills," Harrison argued. "You did what I paid you to do, now you need to get out of his life."

"What if I don't?" Madison asked.

"I don't think you'll have a choice. Tonight, when he lands, I am going to tell him that I paid you and paid you well to keep tabs on him. I am going to tell him that I not only paid for you to tutor him but also to keep him away from the other girls. I would imagine that He'll never want to have anything to do with you after that."

"And I don't think he'll believe you," Madison retorted.

"I'm going to see him off," Madison replied.

"I don't think so. You see, I set up his flight and told him the wrong time. I brought him here an hour ago. His flight left ten minutes ago."

"You're not being very fair, Mr. Fisher," she said.

"I'm just protecting my son from gold diggers like you.".

The next morning Madison felt ill, especially in the mornings. Could it be?

She had to find out, so she went to the pharmacy and picked up one of the tests.

"Here goes," she went up to the counter and paid for the package. The girl behind the counter put it into a bag and stapled the receipt onto it. Madison carried it out to her car.

The instructions on the package told her that she needed to wait until the morning to take the test.

"Great," she said aloud. "I have to wait another day."

In the morning she removed the little calibrated stick from the package and followed the instructions on the package.

One line indicated that she wasn't, but two lines indicated that she was. She followed the directions on the package and looked at the results of the test. Two lines intersected into a plus sign. She was indeed pregnant.

She looked away and closed her eyes. Salty tears stung in her eyes. Excitement that she was going to have Seth's baby, the pain of not seeing Seth again, and the fear of telling her parents what happened washed over her. What was she going to do?

She felt that the first thing she needed to do was to go to Harrison Fisher and tell him that she was pregnant with Seth's child. She hoped that would convince him to allow her to tell Seth about the pregnancy. After all, the child that she was carrying was his grandchild. Surely, he would understand and help her contact Seth with the information.

At the front door of the office of the factory, Madison squared her shoulders. *Here goes*, she thought.

She pushed open the door and there was a counter with a woman sitting behind it. That must be the receptionist, she thought.

She stepped up to the reception desk.

"May I help you?" asked the woman that Madison later learned was Beca.

'Yes, I need to speak with Mr. Fisher. He must see me now."

The receptionist called Mr. Fisher on the desk phone. 'Mr. Fisher, there's a young girl here Miss.. . What's your name? "

"Tell him that Madison Baton is here to see him," she replied. Later, when she looked back on this moment, she could not believe how calm she was.

The receptionist told Madison's name over the phone.

"Tell him it's important that I talk to him," she said.

She spoke into the phone again, listened for a moment, and then turned back to speak to Madison. "He'll see you."

The receptionist came out from behind the desk and led Madison to Harrison's office.

The man was sitting behind the desk and motioned for Madison to take a seat in front of him. Just like Mr. Potter's chair in *It's a Wonderful Life*, his chair was higher than her chair so that he towered over her as soon as she sat in the chair across the desk from him.

"What can I help you with?" Harrison asked.

"I need to talk to Seth. I have something very important to tell him."

"What do you want to tell him?" Harrison asked.

"I really need to tell him personally."

"You know that isn't going to happen, Madison. If you want to tell him something, you'll have to tell me first."

Madison pursed her lips. She didn't want to tell him, but she had no choice if she wanted to speak with Seth. "Alright. I am pregnant with Seth's baby."

Harrison remained straight-faced and showed no expression. She didn't know what to expect him to say, but she didn't expect Harrison's response.

"I'll pay for the procedure," Harrison said quietly after she told him the news.

"Procedure?" At first, Madison was confused, but then she understood he meant to terminate the pregnancy. "No!' There was anguish in her voice. "No, I could never kill my child!"

"Then I don't know how I can help you. I won't let a gold digger ruin his life."

"Seth needs to know."

"Seth must never know," his father said adamantly.

"He must be allowed to make the decision himself," Madison said. "He is an adult and can decide his own future."

"Not going to happen, Missy," if you love him like you say you do, you must let him go. I'll tell you what. I'll give you a job, and if you work until you deliver, I'll pay your maternity bills. I'll do all that only if you agree not to tell Seth about your pregnancy. It will be good for Seth. It would be good for the child."

Madison hesitated.

"Your parents can't afford to support you, right?"

That's when Madison knew that she had no choice. "Alright, when do I start working?"

She started working at the factory as a floor worker on the line.

Of course, Madison's parents weren't happy with the fact that their daughter was unmarried and pregnant, but they supported her in her decision to keep the child and to work for Harrison to support herself and the child.

She worked every day and only took time off to attend her maternity appointments. She was afraid not to. She was afraid that Harrison would not live up to his agreement to pay her medical bills or if he did, that he might try to steal the child from her. Madison worked until the day before she gave birth.

From that time on, she had to work hard for any promotion that she received at the job. When she found that she couldn't move higher in the business unless she had a college degree, she started going to school nights to get her degree.

Now Ryan was seven years old, and old Harrison Fisher was dead. In addition, Seth replaced Harrison as CEO of the business. Madison knew that some people thought that she was given this promotion to management because she was fraternizing with the boss, but she intended to prove that she had earned her place in the business.

6

Madison wanted to put her best foot forward so on Wednesday, she wore a new outfit that she bought Tuesday night after dinner. She wore a tan suit with a green blouse. Her shoes matched the suit. She also had gone to the hair salon where she had her hair trimmed. She felt weird going to the front door that led to the offices rather than through the factory door on the side of the large industrial building.

"Good morning, Beca," Madison said and stopped at the receptionist's desk. "Is Mr. Fisher in yet?" She didn't feel comfortable calling Seth by his first name. *"Best to keep a professional distance from the boss,"* she thought.

A lot had happened over the past few years, and she needed to see where she stood with Seth before they could be on a first-name basis. He may just want to continue the professional basis and that would be fine with her. At least that was what she was telling herself.

"Your office is across the hall from Mr. Fisher's. Your key is the one on my desk," Beca said without raising her head. She wouldn't even stop what she was working on to welcome Madison as a new office employee.

Madison felt the sting of dislike from the older woman who sat behind the desk. She wondered if Beca had wanted the position that Madison now held.

Madison shook her head. She was not going to let Beca's attitude affect her. Instead, she squared her shoulders and went into the office that was assigned to her. The starkness of the room took her aback. She had not expected the room to be completely bare of modern furnishings. In the corner was an old metal filing cabinet. On a metal desk saw an ancient bulky computer screen with the processor under the desk. It didn't even appear to be connected to the internet. She wondered how she was going to be able to do her job without an internet connection. A well-worn desk chair was behind the desk. Next to the desk was an old folding chair.

Madison walked around the desk and sat in the desk chair. She pushed the button that turned on the old computer. It took a few minutes to boot up.

"This is archaic," Madison thought. She must have murmured to herself because after she thought it, a voice came from the office doorway.

"You're right. It is an old computer, and the furniture is sparse." Seth had come to her office. He carried a yellow notepad on a clipboard. A pen was attached to it with a string/

Madison nodded as Seth wrote down something in his notebook.

"I haven't seen one of these since my father got rid of his years ago." Madison touched the keys on the keyboard.

"That's because, as Beca told me, no one has used this room for years. I'll see that you get a new one by this afternoon. Just let me know whatever hardware and software you need, and I'll get it for you. Let me know what else you might need, and we'll see what we can do."

Madison smiled. "I haven't got a clue what software we'll need. I guess I'll need something that coordinates with your desktop. I didn't see any Wi-Fi in here."

Seth nodded. "I've already contacted the IT guy and he's going to take care of it for you. We'll get you set up with Wi-Fi right away. I'll have to get you a laptop as well. There will be times when you will want to work away from the office. You'll need to study the systems and take the tutorials. Knowing your history, I'm sure you'll be up to speed with the systems in no time. Right now, and for the rest of the morning, I would like to go over your job description with you."

"I guess you expect me to act as your assistant."

Seth unfolded the folding chair leaning against the wall.

"Yes," Seth replied, "but I expect that you'll act as more than that. In many ways, you'll be my tutor again."

"I don't know how much of a tutor I will be able to be, but I'll do my best.

"I would expect no less from you, Madison. Let's go into my office and talk over a couple of cups of coffee. You still drink coffee, don't you?" Seth asked as he refolded the chair and leaned it in the place on the wall where he got it originally.

Madison followed him across the hall. The difference between his office and hers was night and day. His office had a large red oak desk with the latest style of a computer on his desk. Around the desk were matching red oak bookcases filled with books and catalogs. He had a beautiful reddish leather ergonomic desk chair and on the side of the desk nearest the door were a couple of leather chairs on castors and two matching cloth couches with decorative pillows. Above each of the couches were landscape paintings. A coffee table separated the two couches.

Seth motioned for Madison to sit on the chair. He went to the coffee maker and poured coffee into two mugs. "Do you still take your coffee with cream and sugar?"

"No, I dropped the sugar a few years back. Now I just drink it with milk."

He put some creamer into a little pitcher and took it and the cups of coffee to the table. He handed one of the coffees to her and the cream to her and then sat down on the couch beside her and sipped the black coffee in the other cup. Madison poured the creamer into the cup and took a sip as well.

"Well, now let's get started. To begin with, I would like to know how the plant employees do their work and have them tell me what changes they would like to see on the job."

"Well, I have heard several talking in the break room that they would like to get the employees stock options rather than a raise. I don't know if everyone agrees with that.

Seth wrote down something on his yellow notepad. "Anything else?"

"Well, like this old computer, some of the production machines are archaic and need to be replaced," Madison replied. "That old machine you saw me fixing yesterday was older than this computer is. Productivity would improve if someone didn't have to fix it all the time."

"That makes sense. It is something I can tell the board so I can get the financing for the improvements," Seth replied. 'They have the final financial word right now."

Madison nodded.

"I have to demonstrate to the board that it's also in the best interest of the stockholders."

Again, Madison nodded.

"How do you think that every employee has been given the best opportunity to improve?" Seth asked.

They discussed each of the management employees and their abilities and inabilities based not only on employee records but also on what Madison knew about each employee. She didn't just relate what she knew about everyone's work life, but their home life as well.

"I hope I learn half as much about the employees as you already know. You're very observant and very insightful."

"I know what I know because I worked on the production line for as long as I did. You can't know people until you've worked with them. Perhaps you should consider working on the floor as a floor employee for a few days. I don't know any better way of getting to know them better than working with them," Madison suggested. "You should put yourself in their shoes for a shift or two."

Seth nodded. "That sounds like a good idea. See, you've already given a great idea of how we can make this business even better. I really would like the way you think."

After lunch, the technician arrived to set up the internet and Madison's new desktop arrived, and the IT person worked to set it up. Her laptop also arrived. Madison spent the afternoon downloading the software onto the handheld machine. By the end of the day, she took her laptop with her so that she could start studying some of the tutorials so she could begin working on ways she thought the business could be improved.

By the end of the day, Madison had not done work for the business, but she had learned a lot about her new job.

As she crossed the parking lot to her old Ford Escort, she thought about all the work she knew that she had ahead of her for the next week. It would take a while before she totally understood what her role in the business was going to be but she was already looking forward to the challenge..

She opened the door to her car and got in behind the steering wheel. She put the key in the ignition and turned the key. Nothing. Not even a click.

"Oh, no," she exclaimed and opened the car door went to the front of the car, and opened the hood of the car she instantly fell because she had no idea what she was looking for.

Madison heard footsteps behind her and then saw a shadow of the person behind her. She turned around to see that Seth had come over to her car. He looked over her shoulder as she bent over the engine.

"Do you know what's wrong?" Seth asked.

Madison shook her head. "I haven't got a clue."

Seth shook his head.

"It looks as though you need a mechanic," Seth said. "As you can guess, I still don't know anything about fixing cars either. They didn't teach us about this in business school, you know."

"Yeah, I didn't see "engine repair" as a subject in the school course catalog. I guess I'll have to call a wrecker and then my mechanic and have it delivered there," Madison sighed. Although she had no idea what the repairs would cost, she reminded herself to feel relieved that she now had a higher income to cover the expense.

"I guess I should better call an Uber to take me home," Madison said.

"No need for that. I can take you."

"No, that's alright. I can take an Uber. You don't have to go to the trouble. Uber's fine." Madison wasn't mentally prepared for Seth to come to her house yet.

"It wouldn't be any trouble," Seth replied. "Do you still live in your parents' house on Elm Avenue?"

"Yes,"

Seth's car was a red Ferrari. Seth unlocked the car door and Madison opened her door and slid onto the white leather seats.

Madison gave her mother a call and asked her to pick up Ryan from school. She did not want Seth and Ryan to meet yet.

As he drove her home he drove along the river. There along the river was an old house. The grounds were overgrown, and the paint was peeling off the side of the house and the garage. The windows in the garage next to the house were broken.

Madison sighed.

"Why the sigh?" Seth asked.

"Oh, it's the old Medford house."

I remember when we used to go there when we were in high school."

Madison sighed again. "Yeah, me too."

"Remember when we went up into the yard to explore the property?"

"Yeah, it's been empty since then." She said. "Do you remember putting your initials in that tree in the back yard."

"I'll bet it's still there."

"Yeah, if the tree hasn't fallen over or been struck by lightning or anything," Madison replied.

"Remember when we looked in the windows?"

"Yeah, I remember seeing that big old fireplace through all those small windows," Madison replied. "I looked up information about the house a few years ago, and I learned that it was one of the first of the grand houses that were built back here when this area was first getting settled."

"I think it's sad that the owners have allowed the ground to go like it has. I always wished I had that house." Madison sighed again. "It could be a grand house again."

"Perhaps someday you'll be able to afford it," Seth said quietly.

"Ha! I'm lucky to be able to have enough money to pay to get the car fixed!" She exclaimed. "The only way I'll ever be able to afford it is if no one ever buys it and the house is falling in."

"You never know!" Seth replied.

"Maybe I should play the lottery," Madison said drily. "That's the only way I would be able to afford to purchase and fix up a house like that."

"You play the lottery?"

"No, of course not," Madison replied. "I'm not that lucky."

"Perhaps you should try it. You never know when your luck will change," Seth replied. "Let's imagine that you did win the lottery. What would you do with the house?"

"Well, I'd live there for sure, and I think I would make it into a bed and breakfast too."

"You'd run it yourself?"

"I don't know about that," she exclaimed. "If I were to continue working for the factory, I guess I would have to find someone who would be willing to run it for me. Perhaps someone like my mother."

Seth turned the Ferrari onto Madison's street. Seth parked the car up in front of the yellow cape cod with green shutters on Elm Avenue. Madison had no reason to be embarrassed with the way Seth saw her parents' house now. Though her father was gone, she and her mother did their best to keep up with the repairs to the house and the yard. The two of them painted the porch and house trim that summer.

As Seth pulled his Ferrari up to the curb in front of Madison's mother's house. A vinyl white picket fence surrounded the yard. Madison didn't hesitate to get out of the passenger seat.

"Thank you so much for the ride," Madison said.

"Perhaps I can come in and say hello to your mom. I haven't seen Diane in so long. I always liked your parents. They were always such special people to me."

Madison wondered how they could have been such special people to Seth, and he yet not have bothered to attend her father's funeral three years ago. She said nothing about that, instead she said.

"Not tonight, Seth," Madison said. "Maybe another time. I need to help Mom get dinner ready."

It wasn't much of an excuse, but it was all she could think of. She wasn't ready for Seth and Ryan to meet yet. She suddenly realized that she had let the "Seth" slip. "I mean, Mr. Fisher."

"There's no need for formality between us," Seth said. "Always feel free to call me Seth. Mr. Fisher was my father."

As she started to close the passenger door of the car, the front door opened, and Ryan stepped out onto the porch. He waved at Madison. At first, she was afraid that he would run down to the car, but before Seth could say anything more, Madison shut the door and ran up the steps. She hoped that Seth didn't get a close look at the boy. If he did, he might deduce the boy's parentage by his age by his size. It would make him wonder, and Madison was not ready for that epiphany to hit Seth.

7

The following morning, Madison stepped out of the shower and wrapped her hair in a towel. She was just starting to put on moisturizer in front of the bathroom sink when the phone rang.

She looked down at her phone, and the screen indicated that Seth was the caller.

"Hello," she said.

"Hi Madison," Seth said. "Can you be ready for me to pick you up in half an hour?"

"Sure," she replied, "but you don't have to do that. I can get an Uber."

"Now we have been through this before," Seth replied. "I'll be there in half an hour. You will be ready, in thirty minutes, won't you?"

Madison's mind thought about the logistics of getting out of the house without Seth seeing Ryan. "Yes, I can make that possible."

She hurried to put on her makeup and do her hair. The clatter of pots and pans in the kitchen indicated that her mother was already making breakfast.

Madison dressed quickly. She put on her favorite blue tee-shirt that said, "Be Happy. What do you have to lose?" Even though she had been promoted, she donned her jeans and old steel-toed work shoes. She wore her usual work clothes because Seth had put business meetings on hold so that Seth and she could work on the floor that day.

After she was dressed, she went to Ryan's room. "Wake up Sleepyhead. Time to get ready for school. Grandma's already making breakfast."

As Ryan brushed his teeth and washed his face, Madison laid out his school clothes.

Half an hour later Madison slid into the heated leather passenger seat in Seth's Ferrari.

"Ooo, this is nice," she snuggled down into the seat's warmth. "I could get used to this."

Seth turned and smiled at her. "It is nice. Isn't it? I hope you don't mind, but I already called your mechanic and he said that he looked at the car before he left the garage last night and he said that the problem is the alternator, and it will cost you. . ." he mentioned an amount.

Madison sighed. She had that much money in the bank, but it was all she would have until payday. At least, she had it.

"He said he'll have your car ready by the end of the day."

"Thank God," Madison replied. "I'm relieved that I will have my car by the end of the day so I can attend my college classes."

"What? You don't like my chauffeuring you around in my Ferrari?"

Madison laughed. Seth still had that way about him where he always seemed to put her at ease. "That's not it. I guess I'm just used to my independence."

"I see," Seth replied. "Does your son go to daycare on a bus or does your mother take him?"

"The bus picked him up fifteen minutes ago. He goes to elementary school," Madison said.

"Oh, I didn't realize he was that old. Is he in kindergarten?"

"No, he's in the first grade."

Madison could have kicked herself. She wished she hadn't let him know that Ryan was old enough to be in school.

In what seemed like just a couple of minutes, but was probably more like fifteen, when they arrived at the factory.

Because Seth wanted to determine the condition of the machine that kept breaking down, they decided that they would evaluate the machine. Seth would take notes of what he learned that day and share the information with the board. He hoped to demonstrate to them that replacing the machine was a necessary investment for the company's bottom line.

Everyone in the company knew that the board was put in place several years ago when Harrison Fisher incorporated the company. He had chosen them because they were as conservative as the old man himself. Their main concern was the bottom line. There was talk of the company stock going public in the future, and the board wanted to keep the business looking good on paper. Making a profit was their main goal.

Seth and Madison worked at the machine all day. Madison operated the machine while Seth timed how fast Madison, who was experienced, managed to put out and then how long it took her to fix it. This was his way of showing the best that this machine could do under the best circumstances. After that, Seth worked as a new employee on the machine and called the mechanics when the machine broke down. Madison held the stopwatch and recorded the times. She counted the machine's performance and downtime. As they worked, they discussed the ways using newer available technology could improve production costs. Seth took copious notes. Because they spent so much time analyzing the machine's performance, a backload of material had piled up in front of the machine by the early afternoon. Madison had run the machine and pushed herself to get the machine's output caught up.

To save time, Seth stood by and helped handle the finished product as it came off the machine. He barely kept up with Madison's work until the machine broke down again, which slowed her progress.

"You certainly know how to run this machine," Seth exclaimed.

"It comes with practice," Madison answered.

By the end of the workday, she had diminished the pile of work that was piled in front of the machine, but the pile beside the machine was still higher than Madison would have liked to leave for the next day.

"Tomorrow, whoever is running this machine will start from behind, but that can't be helped. I'll recommend to Janice that she assign the machine to one of the more experienced workers," Madison replied. "Excuse me while I change my clothes for school this evening."

"Oh, you have classes this evening?"

"Yes, I have a business class every Tuesday and Thursday evening," she replied. "I also have an online class, but I can do that any time during the week."

"I see," Seth seemed to be thinking about something and then said. "Alright. Get changed, and I'll take you to get your car."

"I can call an Uber," she replied.

"Not that again! Don't be ridiculous. I am happy to take you back to the mechanic's shop. It is absolutely no trouble."

Madison knew better than to argue. Seth wouldn't take no for an answer so despite her hesitancy, he drove her to the mechanic's garage. At the mechanic's shop, Madison paid for the work that had been done. She thanked Seth for his help and took her car. She was glad that the car didn't need to stay at the mechanic's any longer than that. Not only because of the in-person business class that evening but also, because she didn't want Seth to find out about Ryan. *Not because she didn't want them to meet,* she told herself she did not doubt that Seth and Ryan would eventually learn of the other's existence.

The in-person class was about the various aspects of business management within a production business, and it seemed timely that they were discussing OSHA regulations that evening.

OSHA regulations were one of those areas where Harrison Fisher had only been concerned when an inspector came to visit the plant when he pushed for employees to make necessary changes to procedures only to return to the same procedural disregard after the inspector's visit. Some of the employees at the plant rumored that a few months earlier, he had even had to pay a fine because not following lock-out tag-out procedures had caused one of his mechanics to suffer damage to one of his hands. Other employees claimed he paid a bribe. Now that she was Seth's assistant, she made a mental note to find out if Harrison had made any fines or bribes to the OSHA inspector.

The OSHA regulations lesson had her head swimming by the time the class ended, and she couldn't wait to get home. She couldn't wait to put her feet up after a busy day at work and a mind-exhausting day in class.

She turned the corner onto her street when she saw the familiar red Ferrari in front of the house. She gasped.

Seth's Ferrari was on the street in front of her parents' house. Seth, her mother, and Ryan were eating ice cream cones on the front porch.

8

All eyes were on Madison as she climbed the porch stairs. Seth and her mother were both poker-faced, but her son's chocolate ice cream-smeared face beamed.

"We bought you hamburgers and fries for dinner, Mom!"

Seth then replied. "Your mother said that you wouldn't mind if I took your mother and Ryan out for burgers, fries, and ice cream."

"Oh, she did, did she," Madison looked at Diane and Diane shrugged. Madison would need to talk to her mother about this later.

"We brought you back a burger and fries, but we weren't able to bring back any ice cream for you because, well, you know."

"Yeah, ice cream melts," Madison said.

"Ryan, come inside with me so we can wash off that chocolate ice cream from your face and hands," Diane said and reached out for her grandson's hand. She smirked at Madison and then beamed a smile at Seth.

Ryan looked over at Seth and Seth shook his head. "You go in like your grandmother says. I think your mother and I have some things to discuss."

"Okay, Dad," Ryan said and went in the front door with his grandmother while looking back at Seth and Madison.

Madison felt her face grow numb. Her jaw dropped. "You know."

"Of course, I know. I don't need a paternity test to know that Ryan is my son," Seth said evenly. "Why didn't you tell me about him?"

"I didn't think. . ." Madison's voice drifted off.

"You didn't think?" Seth was angry. He sounded angrier than she had ever remembered hearing him sound. "I don't understand why you would keep his existence from me!"

"I couldn't!"

"You couldn't? I had suspected as much yesterday evening when I realized how old Ryan had to be, but since you rushed to get away from me, I couldn't 'see him close so I decided to do a little investigating. After I left here, I went back to the factory and looked at your records and saw that his birthday was nine months after I went to Europe."

"I see," Madison lowered her eyes.

"I decided then that I had to check him out for myself. Since it seemed as though you were trying to keep Seth and me apart, I decided to check him out while I knew that you were out of the picture for a while. As luck would have it, you told me that today was the day to find out when you let me know that you were going to be in class this afternoon. Lucky me. Because you told me you had class and wouldn't be here. When I came to your door earlier this evening your mother let me in like I knew she would. Your mother is a good person. She would never let you keep Ryan away from me. I wouldn't have expected that of you either. You surprise me."

"Mom has been telling me to tell you about Ryan."

"You still haven't told me why you tried to keep the fact that he's my son from me."

"I didn't want you to feel obligated for anything. I have taken complete responsibility for his upbringing."

"Obligated? Do you think I feel obligated? I have a son! He's a great kid! What I don't understand is why you tried to keep his existence from me. You knew that I would figure it out eventually. Didn't you? When I checked out the date of his birth and did the math back to when he was conceived, there was little doubt in my mind that I'm his father."

"Who gave you the right to tell him that you are his father?"

"Well, I guess that's a moot point. I *am* his father, and he has a right to know that as much as I do."

"But you could have waited until I was here to tell him. Couldn't you?"

"Don't change the question. You still haven't told me why. How could you refuse to tell me that I had a son or that you were pregnant in the first place?"

"I... I." How could she explain to him that if she didn't keep it quiet that Ryan was Seth's son, that Seth's father would cut Seth off from all his inheritance, and that Madison cared too much about Seth? How could she explain that she didn't feel that she could tell him that now when he was still grieving his father's death? It now seemed like a lame excuse not to tell him about Ryan when they first reconnected. "I really can't say. What are you going to do?"

"I'm Ryan's father and I am going to behave like I'm his father. I expect to be a part of his life. What else can I do? What else did you think I would do?" Seth looked her hard in the eyes and she was the first one to look away. "Do you think that I am such a loser that I would not step up and be a man?"

He then spoke softly. "Right now, I'm going to tell Ryan good night, and then you and I can talk about arrangements tomorrow."

"Arrangements?"

"Yes, but as I said, right now I am going to tell my son good night."

My son," Madison retorted.

"Our son," he said firmly and went into the house. "I'm in his life now and don't you forget it."

"Then what?" Madison asked.

"I'm not sure yet. This has all been so sudden. I have a lot to think about before work tomorrow."

She wondered what he was going to do. Would he take her to court for custody or at least demand joint custody? What would all of this do to their work relationship? Would they be able to continue to work together?

Madison stayed out on the porch while Seth went into the house. She heard Seth's low voice and Ryan's childish voice laughing about some sports figure. She heard Ryan asking him when Seth was going to be back, and he said that he was going to return the next day. She heard Ryan say, "I love you, Dad."

Madison's stomach was tied up in knots. Children were so accepting. She should have been relieved that Seth finally knew and that he accepted Ryan as his son, but she felt dread in the pit of her stomach.

The father and son moved away from the porch door so that she could no longer hear their conversation. Not hearing their conversation, she returned to her own thoughts. *What did he want to talk about? Was he going to confront her further after he came back onto the porch about why she didn't want to tell him about Ryan?*

A few minutes later, the porch screen door squeaked open, and Seth stepped out.

"We have a few things that we need to work out regarding Ryan," he said.

"Such as?" Madison asked. She was ready for an argument. The smile he gave her unnerved her more than anger would have.

"Oh, my God. I'm a father and I didn't know it," he marveled as he still had not fully processed that fact. "I want you to know that I expect to pay my fair share of his expenses," Seth replied.

"I can give him anything he needs," Madison replied.

"That's not the point. I think it's time I pulled my share of his care. I want to start by paying for his health insurance."

"Your father already took care of that. It's one of the benefits of my employment."

"My father knew?"

"Yes, he knew. That's why he gave me a job at the factory," she said.

"And he never told me."

"He didn't want you to know. He. . ."

"He wanted to control my life as usual," Seth said drily. "I see how it is. You and he both wanted to keep Ryan away from me. Well, I'm here now so you'll have to get used to me being in his life."

"I guess, it doesn't matter what we do or don't have between us, we are both Ryan's parents," Madison stepped toward the door and opened the screen.

"You got that right," Seth replied.

Without another word, Seth walked down the porch steps, got in his Ferrari, and drove off.

9

After Seth left, Madison helped Ryan run his bath.

"Dad said he's coming over when I get off school tomorrow!" Ryan said.

Ryan threw his dirty clothes into the clothes hamper and slid into the filled bathtub.

"That's great, Ryan," Madison replied. She took a towel off the towel shelf and set it on the sink. She poured some shampoo into her hand. She then instructed her son to dunk under the water in the tub, and She rubbed the shampoo into his hair.

As she built up the lather in his hair, he said. "Did you know that Dad used to play football, basketball, and baseball when he was in high school?"

"I did," Madison exclaimed. "You and he had a good long conversation. Didn't you."

"He said he would show me his trophies and ribbons and stuff!"

"I know you'll like that," Madison replied.

Ryan went on and on about the things that he and his father discussed while eating burgers, fries, and ice cream. "He even said that he would teach me a few things about football and basketball," Ryan exclaimed. "I'll bet I'll be as good in sports as he is."

"I wouldn't doubt it," Madison replied. "You and he are a lot alike."

He was so excited about having a dad that he hadn't yet gotten onto the topic of why his father was just now arriving in his life. He said that he couldn't wait until the next day at school when he could tell his school friends about the time he spent with his dad.

Madison sighed. Those questions would have to be answered soon enough.

Madison left Ryan in the tub while she went down to the living room where Diane was watching television and crocheting potholders for the church bazaar.

"Mom, why did you let Seth just walk in here and take Ryan out without my permission."

Diane put down her crochet hook, picked up the remote, muted the television, and put the remote down on the table beside her.

"Well, dear," her mother said. "I don't see that I had much choice. I'm just the child's grandmother. Seth is Ryan's father, and he knew it."

"Oh, God, Seth comes back and upsets my whole life!" Madison sunk into one of the living room chairs. She shook her head and lowered her head into her hands. *She felt like she was in a nightmare.*

"I don't know what you are complaining about. Seth seems to be good with Ryan. Consider it a blessing. Do you know how many women would give anything to have the father of their children willing to take care of those children? You were just telling me the other day about how you didn't know how you would be able to afford to raise him. Now Seth is here and willing to help. Consider this a blessing. "

Madison sat up straight in her chair and leaned toward her mother.

"What if he wants to take him from me like his father threatened to do? Or how long do you think Seth gives up on this novelty of being a Dad to Ryan? What if he wants more than to help with his son? What would stop Seth from walking into Ryan's life, and then when he tired of playing 'dad', and he breaks Ryan's heart?"

"It's sound like a lot of "what ifs" to me," Diane replied. "Your heart was broken seven years ago. Perhaps it's time to let it go."

"Who said I was heartbroken?" Madison asked. She raised both hands in a questioning gesture.

"The walls in this house aren't that thick that your father and I didn't hear those nights when you cried over having to be a single parent. I know all about those times you allowed yourself to let go of the pain you were feeling and cry your eyes out."

"Well, so you understand why I want to protect Ryan." Madison looked her mother straight in the eye and Diane stared right back at her.

"Aren't you putting the broken cart before the horse?" Madison's mother asked. "Just because Seth left you all those years ago, doesn't mean that he's going to do the same thing to Ryan. He's eight years older than he was back then. He's matured, I'd say. Not only that, but he also seems to be very kind to you today as well. There was nothing to stop him from telling you that he was sending you back to the factory floor, and yet, that didn't occur."

Madison ran her hands through her hair and shook her head.

"I'm sure that won't last now that he knows the kind of person that he thinks that I am. He knows that I know the production side of the business. He's promoted me for the sake of the business," Madison replied. "However, I'm sure there are a lot of people who could fit the bill. Plus, once he learns all the information that I have to offer, I'm sure he'll just discard me like yesterday's news."

Diane's eyebrows rose. "Are you sure that's the only reason? Do you think that perhaps he wants you back in his life?"

"I'm not sure of anything!" Madison exclaimed. "I'm not sure that Seth won't dump me into the unemployment lines when he's gleaned all the information from me that he can get or that he won't hit me up with papers wanting full custody of Ryan! There always seems to be ulterior motives when it concerns me and the Fisher men!"

Madison stood up so that she towered over her mother. Diane, unwilling to be dominated by her daughter, also stood up.

"I think Seth is a far better person than that," Diane replied. 'From what I have seen so far, Seth is drastically different than his father."

"I don't think he could have felt about me the way that I felt about him all those years ago. He got married just two years after he went to Europe."

Seth had married a woman named Bianca. It was then that Madison felt consigned to the idea that Seth was going to come back to her.

"And that marriage didn't last," Diane replied. "Don't forget that."

"Mom, I'm done! I'm ready for bed!" Ryan called from the top of the stairs to let her know that he was ready for her to tuck him in.

Madison went to the doorway and turned back toward her mother who had again picked up her crocheting.

"I hope you're right," Madison replied and went up the stairs to put her son to bed.

10

Madison wasn't sure what to expect when she arrived at the plant the next day. She half expected to find Seth at her office ready to send her back to the assembly line. When she came into the hallway where their offices were, her office door stood open and Seth's office door was closed.

She looked over at Seth's office and through the office windows she saw that he was already on the phone. She wouldn't have been surprised if he was on the phone with his lawyer to begin custody procedures. There were so many directions that this could go, and she could drive herself crazy thinking about all of Seth's options when it came to Ryan.

Once in her office, she wasn't sure what she was expected to do so she started studying one of the tutorials about the programs her computer shared with Seth's. While she was watching the tutorial, she wrote down any potential improvements that they could make in the equipment that they had that had regular maintenance problems. After that, she examined the OSHA regulations to see which ones indicated that certain machines needed updates in their security equipment. Then, based on what she read, she decided to take a tour of the factory to see what violations she could find that management needed to address. A meeting with the managers afterward might also be in order.

She picked up the notes that she had prepared and went out onto the floor to do an impromptu inspection. As she toured the plant, she noticed a pallet of boxes in the center aisle. She went to one of the material handlers. He was using a hand truck to move a pallet.

"Hey Mark, as soon as you're done there, can you move that pallet of boxes off the aisle? Leaving anything in the aisle is an OSHA violation."

"No problem, Madison," he said. He lowered the pallet on the hand truck and immediately did as Madison had asked.

Madison smiled. *That wasn't hard*, she thought. She felt a little uneasy about the power that she now had regarding her co-employees even if the position was short-lived. Her life was changing so fast and yet everything and everyone around her were the same. The other employees' lives continued as they had always been and yet Madison's was changing in ways that frightened and even confused her. She wondered how much time would pass before this was all just routine.

As she inspected the factory floor, she saw one of the mechanics working on a machine where the lockout/tagout had not been put into place.

"Hey, Wallace, you forgot to use the lockout tag out before tearing down the machine."

"It's alright. I'll just be working on this for a few minutes."

Madison shook her head. "We haven't had an accident here in two weeks, and I don't want you to be the next."

Madison took the tag from the mechanic's bag and showed the mechanic that she was putting the tag on the breaker box.

"Thanks, Madison," he said.

"Don't remove it until you are done," she reminded him.

He gave her a mock salute. He seemed to be mocking her and yet he didn't argue. Madison wondered if Wallace might be a problem in the future.

Next, she went by the restroom and saw that the janitor was mopping the floor. This young man was several years younger than she was and had just been hired shortly before Harrison Fisher's death. He was the son of one of the machine operators who had been working there longer than Madison had been around.

The janitor had covered a large part of the floor but had not put up any wet floor signs.

The janitor had also failed to put up the wet floor sign in the restroom he had also just cleaned. She went and got several wet floor signs and set them up.

"Thanks, Madison," the janitor replied.

"You should have had those up already," Madison replied. "We don't need falls to occur here. Please remember to make sure to put up signs from now on."

The janitor rolled his eyes.

"You do realize that I can keep you or fire you. Don't you?"

"What? "

"You heard me," Madison replied. She wasn't sure that as Seth's assistant, she could fire one of the employees, but she did know his manager, Roger, and she could impress on him that this young man could be trouble if he didn't respect the authority put in place in the plant.

"So, how's the new position going?" Janice, her former manager, asked her. She carried a clipboard as well. Her clipboard had to do with the products that needed to be completed for the next few shipments.

"To be honest, sometimes I feel overwhelmed," Madison admitted.

"Oh, I'm sure you'll do fine," Janice exclaimed. "I see you've been getting onto some of the men who haven't been keeping up with OSHA regulations.

"Yeah, it is weird being part of the administration team. There's so much to learn," Madison confessed. "I'm not sure how much I can offer Seth except to introduce to him how we do things and perhaps suggest some of the ways that we might be able to improve them."

Behind her back, one of the newer assembly workers named Darcy whispered loud enough for Madison to hear.

"What do you want to bet she's sleeping with the boss?" Darcy said.

Janice heard what Darcy said too and said to Madison. "You know she's just jealous. She has no idea what you've had to put up with to get to where you are now."

Janice was one of the few people that she worked with who knew that Seth was Ryan's father and that Harrison kept a tight thumb on Madison's ability to get promoted.

It was at that moment that Seth entered the factory floor. He was wearing factory work clothes. He no doubt heard what the girl had said and what Janice had said. Rather than saying anything about what had transpired, he said. "I see you've been inspecting the plant," Seth said. "Are you ready to show me where you want me to start working today?"

He had a poker face. It seemed like he was not even letting anyone know his reaction to the fact that he had just found out that he was Ryan's father.

Darcy lowered her head and went back to work.

"I think we need to talk to human resources about repeating some safety training," Madison said. "There are some places where people haven't been paying attention to safety measures."

Seth nodded then replied. "Sounds like you've been busy already this morning. Let's take your notes back to the office, go over what you've got, and then let's get back out onto the floor and see what we can find to do."

Madison nodded. "All right, I'll show you where you can start."

They walked together back to Seth's office. Seth held the door open to allow Madison to walk through the door ahead of him. When the door closed, Seth said. "How was Ryan this morning?"

He motioned Madison to sit down in the chair beside the office couch.

"Excited that you're coming to see him tonight," Madison replied.

A smile tugged at the corner of Seth's mouth. "I'm glad to hear that."

"And I'm glad you're glad," Madison said. "I agree that it's time."

Seth waved off continuing the conversation. "I could talk about Ryan all day, but I think it's important that we keep our business dealings separate from our private life. Let's not talk about Ryan here at work. I think it would be better for everyone involved if we focused on the business while on the clock. We've got a factory to run."

She couldn't agree more. It would make it easier for her as well to compartmentalize their relationship such as it was to non-work hours.

Madison was surprised by what Seth said next. "I think that rather than discussing this with the HR manager, I think that you should hold a meeting with the plant managers this afternoon about letting them handle OSHA regs with the employees. What we need is a safety officer, but right now, we can't afford to hire one."

Madison nodded. She wasn't in accounting, but if Seth said it was true, she had to believe him. She did have to question one thing though. "I thought that you were going to work the floor today."

"I am," he said. "I'm dressed for it, aren't I? I want you to run the meeting with the plant managers."

"Me? I can't do that!' she exclaimed.

"Sure, you can," Seth replied. "I'm sure that you can do it as well as I can."

"But I'm just your assistant," she argued.

"Right, and since I am going to be working on the floor, I need you to assist me by running this meeting."

"But what would I say?"

Seth shrugged. "Just share what you found in your floor inspection and then share what the OSHA law says and tell them that you expect them to follow it. It's that simple. In addition, I want you to prepare a checklist for each manager for their area and explain to them that they are responsible for making sure that the safety checklist is consistently followed. I also want you to make sure that they follow the protocol."

"Why would they listen to what I say? Just a few days ago, I was listening to their instructions."

"Well, then tell them that I expect them to follow it," Seth replied.

"Okay. I think I'll need a script though."

"Fine, you write a script. You've got the rest of the morning to take care of that. You can do that right after you show me where you think I should work today. Where do you think would be the best place for me to begin my factory training?"

She went across the hall to her office and dropped her notebook on her desk. "Let's start with shipping and handling."

"May I ask why there?"

"Because you'll see the beginning of the process and the end of the process. You'll see raw materials coming in and the finished process going out."

"That's brilliant!" Seth exclaimed. "Now let's go to the receiving and shipping department and introduce me to the head of that department."

Madison and Seth walked together to the loading dock. As they came to the loading dock, they saw a gentleman with graying hair poking out from under his yellow hard hat.

The man must have heard the two of them coming because he turned toward them.

"Pete's the shipping manager, Mr. Fisher. You've met Mr. Fisher, haven't you, Pete?"

"Of course, I remember Seth here. I have worked for your father for thirty years," Pete replied and gripped Seth's hand in a hardy handshake. "You were just graduating high school when I saw you last."

"I remember," Seth replied.

"Are you here to supervise how we do things around here?" Pete asked.

"No," Madison answered. "Seth's here to learn the business by getting his hands dirty."

"Good, good, now that's what I like to hear. Your father, rest his soul missed a lot by not being more hands-on," Pete said.

Madison continued. "Since he hasn't worked here as a laborer before, train him to work here just as though he were a new employee. Since you're in charge of both the shipping and receiving, I would like you to teach him what you would any other employee that you assigned to both aspects of your department."."

Pete looked at Madison and then looked at Seth. "You let her get away with that?"

Seth chuckled and nodded. "Yes, she's boss for the day, and if I don't miss my guess, maybe all next week as well."

Pete pursed his lips and nodded. "Well, I would say the factory is in good hands then. Since your dad died, the only other person who knows production in this factory through and through is Madison here."

"I think you might be right. A lot of people have told me that already."

"Have you ever handled a forklift?" Pete asked.

Seth shook his head. "I can't say that I have."

"Then we'll just let you manage a pallet jack and a dolly today, Pete then turned to Madison. "So, how long will I have his help?"

"Just today, but all day," Madison replied. "He'll not only need to know how to unload a truck, but he'll need to know the rudimentary basics of your computer system as well. He needs to know every aspect of the job."

Pete nodded. He turned and motioned to Seth to follow him. "Alright, let me show you around."

Pete handed Seth a hard hat and he led him toward the shipping dock. Madison headed back toward the office, but first, after leaving Seth in Pete's good hands, Madison went to the floor to let the managers of the various departments know that she wanted a meeting with them after lunch. Back at the office, she then created a list that she would go over with them. After that, she created the checklists for each department.

Frank Carter, the manager of the maintenance department, was the only one to ask if Seth would be at the meeting.

"No, he left me in charge for the day," Madison replied. "He's going to be working as a lumper in shipping."

"Wow, that's a switch," Frank said. "I am impressed."

After letting the managers on the floor know about the meeting that afternoon, she told Beca about the meeting after lunch.

She then sat down to write the agenda for the meeting. Once the agenda was written, made copies of it. She took out her lunch bag and juice from the lunchroom and was eating her lunch when Seth came in from shipping and receiving.

"Oh, I didn't realize you brought your lunch," Seth replied. "I just called for a pizza."

"Thanks anyway," Madison said as she bit into her ham and cheese sandwich.

"It's Hawaiian, your favorite," Seth replied.

"You remember that I like ham and pineapple on my pizza?" Madison replied.

"I remember a lot about you," he said.

"I'm afraid I'll have to pass. I have my sandwich," Madison said and took another bite of her ham and cheese. She didn't know why she suddenly felt self-conscious.

An uncomfortable silence fell between them.

After what seemed like an eternity, Seth said. "Are you sure you don't want any?"

Her mouth was full of sandwiches. Therefore, Madison just shook her head.

Seth went out to the reception area where he must have invited Beca to join him for pizza because she followed him back to his office. The HR manager came in a few minutes later and took a couple of pieces as well. He also invited the HR manager to a couple of pieces as well. The pizza smelled awesome and Madison's mouth watered. She had not had Hawaiian pizza in a long time. She regretted her decision not to partake of the pizza with ham and pineapple, but she wouldn't change her mind now.

After lunch, the floor managers came to Madison's office, and she went over the OSHA violations that she had seen that morning.

She learned from some of the managers who had been in their positions for many years that Seth's father had been known to pay off the inspectors when there had been indiscretions during the inspection.

He seemed to only care about the business's bottom line and not for the safety of the employees so paying off the OSHA official was something that he probably felt was cheaper than following some OSHA laws. Though there had been some minor safety accidents, he had been lucky there had been no major ones.

"Now, I know that things have been lax around here for the past few years regarding OSHA regulations, but we're changing that. The safety of our co-workers is my number one priority."

"What about Seth's priorities? Is he going to undermine this decision of yours when he finds an expense that doesn't suit the board of directors?" Janice asked.

"Well, I do not doubt that Mr. Fisher is in total agreement. He's the one who wanted me to have this meeting with you this afternoon about this subject."

She handed out flyers containing information about the OSHA regulations that were likely to be monitored in the factory. She then handed out checklists to each of them.

She then gave her presentation. When she finished, she asked the managers what changes they would like to see in the business overall. Seth had not asked her to do this, but Madison thought that perhaps having the list would help him understand better what the staff wanted and needed in their respective departments.

Now, mind you, this is just a wish list that you have for your departments. I also plan to put a suggestion box out on the floor for all the employees. The more input we have, the better we'll be able to serve the employees in their service to our customers.

She wrote down everything that they suggested. Some of the ideas that they came up with, Madison thought were frivolous, but others she thought bordered on genius. She wondered if Seth would see it the same way.

She agreed to give the information to Seth when he finished working throughout the plant. She hoped that he would not be upset because she had done more than he had expected of her.

For the rest of the afternoon, Madison designed a suggestion box of cardboard to hang up in the breakroom if Seth approved her suggestion box.

11

After she finished the suggestion box, Madison went to the front desk where Beca was answering the phones. As Beca hung up the phone and turned toward Madison, Madison remarked how impressed she was that Beca was at answering the phone and explaining to the callers that Mr. Fisher would call him later that day.

"I'm good at my job," Beca replied. "I've worked for Mr. Harrison Fisher for longer than you have worked at this plant. Truth be known, I should have been offered the job you now hold. You know little about running this factory."

"You certainly know what to say on the phone," Madison replied. "I'm glad that you're the one fielding these calls. I don't know that I would know what to say."

Madison wasn't trying to butter Beca up. Madison knew that Beca did know a lot about the business and having her on her side would be to her advantage. Beca was older than Madison by several years, but she could imagine that she was not much different than other women at the plant who would have done anything to have Madison's job. Therefore, as Seth's assistant, she needed to be careful what she said to other employees.

However, she had no idea how she would be able to get on the receptionist's good side. Seth had his reasons for choosing Madison for the job, and her job was to do the best she could with the position. She hoped that she had not overstepped her bounds by creating the suggestions box.

At the end of the day, Seth knocked on Madison's door.

"How did the job go?" she asked looking up from the report she was creating.

"Pete's great to work for. A nice guy. He even taught me how to run the forklift. He said I was a natural, even though I am sure that he only said it because I was the boss."

"I hear a but coming," Madison replied.

"Yes, there is a but. I know he wouldn't complain, but that computer he is using is archaic!"

"Yes, your father didn't want to change much."

"Change costs money," they said in unison.

Then Madison continued, "I think it was because he thought that technology got in the way of his control of the place."

"And it has cost us customers," he replied. "We need to get that computer system replaced right away!" he exclaimed.

"I think you should reconsider that idea," Madison said.

"Why do you say that?"

"I think you should wait because Pete plans to retire within the next six months. I suggest that you put Pete's antiquated computer system on a list of things that need to be changed, but please don't make it a priority."

"Oh, I get it. It doesn't make sense to force Pete to learn a new system when he's not going to be around much longer."

"Exactly. I think it's better to train his replacement on a new computer system and then when Pete retires, the new guy will be able to step right in and take over."

"Someone who has been trained on the computer system before Pete ever retires."

Madison pointed at her nose. "Ding ding ding, the boss gets the prize."

"So how did your meeting go with the managers."

"It went well," Madison replied. "At first they weren't sure that you would back up the OSHA rules that we are supposed to follow."

"Are you telling me that those federal laws weren't always followed?"

Madison didn't know how to put the subject delicately. "That's right. Sometimes inspectors were even paid off."

"I see," Seth's lips pursed into a straight line. "Did they say any-thing else?"

"Well, they did have some suggestions," Madison replied. "I kind of asked them to share them."

"Really, what suggestions did they offer?"

Madison took the notes she had written and handed them to him. "There are some that are too personal to consider, but others are really good."

Seth looked over Madison's notes and nodded. "I think you've done well. We'll have to keep these suggestions in mind."

"I also prepared a suggestion box," Madison replied. "I thought it would create more loyalty within the business if we brought the employ-ees into the decision-making process."

"Go ahead and put up your suggestion box. I agree that it will help learn where the employees' heads are and possibly gain some new insights that we didn't have before."

"Thank you," Madison replied. "I'm glad you are pleased."

I'm amazed at how well you know the employees here, Madison," Seth replied. "I'm surprised my father didn't realize what a gem he had in you."

"He didn't like me very much," Madison replied. "I was the girl who tried to trick her way into the Fisher family."

"Because you had Ryan?" Seth said softly.

"Ding ding ding, give the boss another prize," Madison said drily.

"What I can't understand is why you were still willing to work for him for so long. From what I could see from your personnel file he over-looked your requests for promotion several times. He was foolish in his prejudices.

Madison shrugged. "It's all water under the bridge. We're still on the clock, and as you said, we can't mix business with our personal lives."

"Alright, we'll talk about it later," Seth eyed her suspiciously, "but we *will* talk."

12

∾

Seth drove directly from work to the Baton house. He drove his car and Madison followed him in hers. As soon as Ryan saw Seth's Ferrari, he ran to meet them. Madison expected Ryan to greet her like he usually did, but instead, Ryan ran up to hug Seth. She seemed invisible to him.

Ryan hugged Seth around the waist.

"Aren't you going to say hello to your mother?" Seth asked. Ryan sighed and gave Madison a half-hearted hug.

At first, Madison felt hurt that Ryan had dissed her for Seth, but then her rational mind took over. *Of course, he was happy to have a man in his life who enjoyed sports like he did. Ryan was just excited to finally get to know his father.*

Ryan then turned his attention back to Seth.

"Can you show me how to hold a football? How about throwing a baseball with me? Do you think we can go to a football game together?"

"We probably could do all those things, but we can't do them all tonight. How about we shoot some hoops before dinner tonight, "Seth asked.

"Yeah!" Ryan exclaimed. "Woohoo!"

He punched the air. Madison had never seen him so excited to get to know anyone.

"Give me a minute and I'll change out of these steel-toed boots and put on my tennis shoes."

Seth opened the trunk of his car and pulled out a box with new tennis shoes that were still in their original box. He laced them up and put them

76

on. He had not been on the basketball court in a while and bought the shoes specifically because of Ryan.

Madison went into the house where her mother was looking out the window toward the garage where Seth and Ryan were shooting at the basketball hoop. The basketball hoop was an old one that Madison had purchased at a yard sale and had hung it herself. She remembered how she had to go on Google to find out how high the basketball goal was supposed to be.

"They certainly are getting along well," Diane exclaimed.

"Yes, they are," Madison replied.

"How did things go at work?" Diane eyed her daughter's reaction to the question.

"It was fine," Madison murmured.

"Just by the way you said fine, it doesn't sound like it was 'fine'.

"It's just weird is all. I mean he treats me politely and all, kind of like he did when I first became his tutor. He's keeping me at arm's length."

"What do you expect? It's been almost eight years since you saw him last. He's coming around."

"Yes, because of Ryan."

"He hired you as his personal assistant before he knew there was a Ryan. That should account for something. I always found him to be a nice boy."

"Yes, until you found out that I was pregnant."

"You both lied to me and your father the night that you, well, you know," Diane exclaimed.

"Yeah," Madison and Diane both looked out the window and watched Ryan make a basket. Ryan jumped up and down and Seth gave him a high-five."

"They really do seem to get along well," Diane replied. "A boy that age needs a man in his life. I always thought it would be your father, but. . ."

"Yeah," Madison said aloud.

Diane made a little choking noise and then brushed a tear from her eye. "I'm just glad Seth is here for him now."

An uneasy feeling came over Madison that she didn't quite recognize.

She felt at a loss. She felt like she used to have back before she met Seth. She recognized it. Envy had raised its ugly head again. Why was she jealous? She was jealous because Seth was now dominating Ryan's thoughts. Something deeper told her that wasn't exactly where her jealousy originated, but she didn't want to press down into those feelings right now. She'd have to sort out all that later because Seth and Ryan were on their way into the house.

"Thanks for a great time, Dad," Ryan exclaimed. "Can we do it again tomorrow? It's Saturday. You know."

"Would you like to stay for dinner tonight?" Diane asked as she put some of her homemade dinner rolls on the table.

"I'm sorry. I can't" Seth exclaimed.

"It was one of your favorites., ham with macaroni and cheese," Diane said.

"I'd like to, but I have to get home and shower," Seth replied. "Between working at the factory and playing basketball with Ryan, I am a little rank."

"Ah, Dad, do you have to go?" Ryan continued asking Seth about when they could do all kinds of things together.

"Hey, Sport," Seth said. "We'll see each other tomorrow. We have all the time in the world to do all kinds of things together. I'm not going anywhere soon. You can count on that."

That word '*soon*' stuck in Madison's mind and heart like a knife. He had been at her side long enough for her to fall for him but ended. *Would Seth do the same to Ryan when he grew tired of playing 'dad'?*

13

Ryan was dressed and ready for Seth's arrival the next morning. He pressed his face to the glass in the screen of the door watching to see when Seth's Ferrari would drive up in front of the house.

"He's here!" he exclaimed. He opened the front door and met Seth on the sidewalk. He took his hand and walked with him up onto the porch.

As he came up onto the porch, he saw Madison in the kitchen spreading butter on toast. "Would you like something for breakfast?" Madison asked. She offered her piece of toast to him. " It's Mom's homemade apple butter. I remember how you like it."

"You sure know how to tempt a guy. I would love some toast with your mom's apple butter!" She handed him the piece that she buttered and put two more slices of bread in the toaster.

"If you're going shopping, perhaps you should take Madison's car," Diane said as she came into the kitchen. She had a basket of dirty laundry on her hip.

"Good idea," Seth replied. "You can drive, Madison."

"I didn't know that I was coming with you," Madison replied.

"Of course, you're coming with us," Seth exclaimed. "We're getting Ryan some new clothes. I'm sure you know Ryan's sizes and what he needs better than I do."

Madison almost objected to Seth spending money on clothes for Ryan. She had always paid for his care up to this point, but in the end, she didn't say anything. Why shouldn't Seth buy Ryan some clothes? He was, after all, his father.

"Okay." Madison wasn't sure that she liked the idea of spending the day with Seth, but she was glad to be able to go with them. At least she knew that Seth wouldn't try to take custody of Ryan if she was with them, and they were in her car. "My car has more storage space anyway."

Madison could have kicked herself. She didn't want to sound like a gold digger who hinted that he should fill her car with clothes for Ryan.

Seth didn't react to what Madison had said and the three of them climbed into her car. Seth and Ryan sat in the backseat so that they could sit together.

"So, where do you think that we should go to get you some clothes."

"The Sports Shop!" Ryan exclaimed. The Sports Shop was an exclusive shop that sold high-end sports memorabilia including shoes and clothing.

"Then The Sports Shop it is!" Seth replied.

Madison had started the car but had not yet moved it. "I don't know. That store is expensive."

'Oh, I'm not worried about the cost," Seth replied. "I am sure that I can afford whatever Ryan wants and needs."

Normally Madison bought Ryan's clothes online and always looked for bargains, but since Seth insisted on taking Ryan to this high-end sporting goods store to buy him high-top sports shoes that Madison would never have afforded to buy the seven-year-old who grew faster than he could wear out clothes, Madison could not object.

While in the store, Ryan talked him into buying him several T-shirts and hoodies of both their favorite sports teams. He bought himself a hoodie that matched the one that Ryan had picked out. He also bought Ryan the best quality sports gear including a new basketball goal that had the new netting and basketball.

'We'll put up the new basketball hoop after we get home," Seth said.

They also bought athletic pants. They then went to another store where they picked out some top-of-the-line jeans, athletic socks, and sports related. By the time they were done, the entire trunk was full as was most of the backseat where Ryan and Seth sat. Even more packages were piled on the front seat.

"I'm hungry. Where should we go for lunch, Ryan?" Seth asked as they got into the car.

"Pizza!" Ryan exclaimed. He named a specific kid's-oriented pizza place.

"Pizza it is then!" Seth said.

Madison pulled up in front of the brightly colored Kids Pizza Palace. Ryan held onto his father's hand as they walked into the restaurant.

Inside the restaurant kids ran everywhere and chaos ensued. Children who seemed to have more energy than they could control ran hither and yon around the children's arcade games and the buffet of various types of pizzas, salad fixings, and desserts.

Ryan wanted to go play some of the arcade games, but Seth convinced him that they needed to eat first. They went through the buffet line and took a seat in a booth with bright red-colored seats. As they were eating, a tall boy with messy blonde hair came in with his mother. Madison knew that the boy's mother worked in the kitchen at Ryan's school, but Madison did not know her personally.

The woman seemed worn out, and the boy was begging to immediately play the games.

"It's James! Ryan exclaimed and he then turned to Seth. "I go to school with him!" He couldn't help but let his friend know his latest news. "Hey, James. This is my dad! Come meet my dad!"

James' mother called for him to get in line, but James ignored her and ran over to Ryan. "Hey, Ryan. Are you telling me that this is your dad?"

"Yeah," he said to James and then turned to Seth. "Dad, this is my friend James Emerson."

"Nice to meet you, James," Seth said to James. "How about you get in line with your mother and if it's okay with her, you can come and sit in our booth."

Madison said nothing because this outing was for Ryan's benefit. She watched as James told his mother what Seth had said. James' mother looked over at Seth and smiled a weary smile and mounted the words 'thank you'.

James quickly went through the line and as his mother paid for their meal, James ran over to the table where the two boys talked about the food they had on their plates. James' mother sat in a chair at the end of the booth and Seth sat in the booth beside. Madison.

After they ate their food, James asked his mother for money for the arcade games. Before she could say anything, Seth offered to give both boys the money they wanted to play the games. As they left to play their games, James' mother moved from the chair to the other side of the booth.

"So, you're Ryan's father?" James' mother asked.

"Yes, I am," Seth said without hesitation. "I'm Seth Fisher."

James' mother put out her hand to Seth "Hi, I'm Christine Emerson".

Seth smiled. "Nice to meet you, Christine."

"How come Ryan didn't tell us about Seth before?" she asked Madison.

"He didn't know until just a couple of days ago," Madison replied.

"So, are you seeing each other again?" James' mother asked Seth.

Before Seth said anything, Madison spoke up.

"No," Madison replied. "He's just my boss."

James' mother's face lit up. "Really?"

Madison felt a sinking feeling in her chest as she realized Christine Emerson's interest in Seth Fisher was more personal than she was letting on. Christine Emerson was a single mother just as Madison was. Her husband had run off with a barfly from the local bar. Although he was legally obligated, he was not paying child support. This meant that Christine was now in the market for another husband and father for her boy.

Madison knew that she should be feeling that it didn't matter, but for some reason it did. She decided that it was because now that Seth had come into Ryan's life, she didn't want Ryan to be disappointed if Seth suddenly stopped coming by to see him, at least, that was what she told herself.

The boys played games for an hour or so. Seth was attentive as Christine told them about how she wanted to get into sales. Seth handed her a business card and suggested that she try getting a sales position at his plant. He said that he would soon be in the market for more salespeople.

Christine was thrilled with the prospect of working for Fishers.

Christine had shopping to do so she couldn't stay long. Ryan gave a reluctant goodbye to his friend and then rejoined his parents.

"Are you ready to go Sport?" Ryan asked. "When I was your age, my bedroom was filled with sports memorabilia. What do you say we buy you a comforter set with your favorite sports team for your bed?"

Ryan looked at him quizzically and didn't seem to know what he meant.

"Do you know where they might sell those, Madison?" Seth asked.

"I know just the place,"

Madison drove them to another store where they had sports bedding sets along with other sports memorabilia. Seth encouraged Ryan to pick out a comforter, sheets, and pillowcases to put on his bed. He picked out a set of his favorite football team. He also bought him a new lamp to match the bedding. By then Ryan yawned several times and soon dozed off. He cradled his latest purchase.

When they arrived at Madison's mother's house, Ryan awoke ready for another round with Seth.

"Dad, could you help me make my bed?" he asked.

Seth looked toward Madison, and Madison nodded.

"Alright," what else could she say? Seth seemed to want to make up for lost years, and who was she to deny him that?

As Seth went upstairs with Ryan, Madison went out to the porch. As often happened after Labor Day, there was already a nip in the air but not so much of one that she felt she needed a coat.

She sat out on the porch swing and leaned back as she listened to the evening crickets. She remembered how she and Seth used to sit on this porch as she quizzed him about whatever subject they had been studying. That had been a long time ago. Funny that she should think of that now.

Madison watched as Baker Adams walked his dog down the street.

Baker waved. "Hey Madison! Beautiful night, isn't it?"

"Yeah," Madison said back. "I need to enjoy this while I can. Fall weather will be here any day now."

"It sure will! I'm certainly not looking forward to frosty mornings,"

Baker replied. At that moment his dog tugged on his leash and dragged the man down the street.

At that moment, Seth came out onto the porch. "Was that Mr. Adams?"

"Yes, and his youngest dog. He still hasn't learned to keep his dogs from trying to run away from him when he was walking them."

"Some things never change," Seth said. He sat down on the porch swing beside Madison and laid his arm across the back of the swing just as he used to do when they were in high school.

Madison felt uncomfortable with his arm along her shoulders, so she scooted to the far end of the porch swing. Seth looked at Madison and then at his arm and lowered his arm down to his side.

You said that you were going to tell me why you continued working at the factory even though my father treated you so badly." Seth leaned forward to listen intently to what she had to say.

"I went to see your father to try to get him to let you know that I was pregnant. At first, he offered to pay for an abortion."

"Which you obviously didn't get," all the color went out of Seth's face.

Madison imagined that Seth was thinking what would have happened if Madison had agreed to an abortion. He would not have experienced that day that they had just spent with Ryan. He would never have known Ryan at all because Ryan never existed.

Madison shook her head. "I refused."

"Can I ask you what your thought process at the time was?"

"To me, the baby was a person that I was responsible for," Madison replied. She didn't want to say that what had been thinking was that the baby would remind her of Seth so she couldn't... wouldn't...

"And what did my father have to say about that?"

"He said that he would pay for my maternity bills. When I said I couldn't be bought, he said that if I insisted on being stubborn and did not agree to what he said he would spend every dollar he had to take the baby from me. He said that he wouldn't do anything if I agreed not to tell you that I was pregnant with your child and worked for him."

"He didn't want me to know, because he wanted to maintain control of my life," Seth shifted his weight as he turned and looked Madison in the eyes.

Madison shrugged. "He was probably just trying to do what he thought was in your best interest."

"He did what was in his interests!" Seth tensed up. "How could he keep me from getting to know my son all these years? How could you agree to something so heinous? Didn't you think that I would want to know my son?"

"I didn't know what you'd think. I wasn't going to force you to do anything that you didn't want to do."

"You could have contacted me and let me know. I would have done what I could to give Ryan what he needed."

"I was afraid that he would take me to court to take Ryan from me. I wasn't going to let your father do that!"

"I'm sorry. I guess I can understand your position at the time. You were between a rock and a hard place. I get it. You were barely out of high school and had to raise our son alone."

"That's not true I didn't have to raise him alone," Madison replied. "I had my parents to help me."

"Thank God for your parents. You've done a fine job raising Ryan and I guess I should be grateful."

"He's my son too, you know," Madison said softly.

"Yes, I haven't forgotten," he said.

At that moment Diane came out to the porch carrying a tray of drinks.

"So, what are you going to do?" Diane asked as she brought ice teas to the small table on the porch."

"I guess we'll have to figure something out. Now that the cat's out of the bag, I can hardly refuse to let you see him. Can I?" Madison said.

"I agree," Seth said. "I think that at least for now, I should continue to come here regularly to get to know him better. Perhaps I can pick him up from school and bring him home."

"That would be helpful," Madison replied. "It would make it easier for Mom on the days that I have to go to school in the evening if you picked him up."

It suddenly occurred to Madison that he used the words 'for now'. *What did he mean by that?*

"I want to help supply groceries for meals as well," Seth replied.

"Oh, that's not necessary, Seth. You're welcome to have meals at our home anytime," Diane said.

"Oh, but I insist on helping with groceries. I'd be happy to take my turn bringing Ruam to and from school too," Seth replied. "It's the least I can do. I have seven years of child support to make up for. I have a lot of catching up to do."

Madison suddenly felt like she was losing control of the situation. She had spent the past eight years getting control over her life. Now it seemed as though Seth was taking control, and she didn't like it.

14

On Sunday evening, Madison read through her reading assignment for school and saw that the class was about the various types of insurance that factories offered. Madison thought that perhaps she would combine her schoolwork with looking over the company's insurance programs and looking for ways to improve them. She would talk to Kayla Raymond on Monday. Kayla was the head of the human relations department of the company, so Kayla probably knew more about the company's insurance programs than anyone.

Monday morning as she was getting ready for work, Madison thought about her conversation with Seth the night before and about how he and Ryan were getting along.

She suddenly felt the resentment that she felt the day before. At first, she thought that she felt her resentment was from the fact that Ryan's attention was so much on Seth and not so much on her.

She knew she shouldn't feel that way, but there was that feeling that her son, the son that she had raised without Seth's help for the past seven years, so quickly attached himself to Seth and wanted only to be with his father. Madison was no longer the center of his world. Seth had taken her place.

She knew she shouldn't feel that way, but she couldn't help it. She had always been protective of him and now he barely acknowledged her existence. He used to hug her at every turn, but now he only gave her an obligatory hug when she asked him for one. Her boy was growing up even if Seth had not come into the picture, Ryan would have still stopped hugging her like a little boy. It just happened sooner than she would have preferred.

It was rather paradoxical because not only did she resent Ryan wanting to spend time with Seth so much, but she also resented the fact that Seth wanted to spend time with Ryan too. She should be happy that Seth enjoyed time with Ryan, shouldn't she?

She felt as though she was quickly becoming one of those utility parents. She was the utility parent, but didn't Seth say that he would take on some of the responsibilities of the boy's care? Didn't he agree to help take care of his son's needs and even agree to go with Madison to buy school clothes for him.?

However, there was something that did not ring true about this supposition that Madison did not yet understand. She couldn't put her finger on what it was, but it was there just below the surface.

Madison did as she had done on Friday and worked in the office while Seth worked on the floor. This time he worked with the staff on the production floor.

Madison made her way down the hall to the human resources offices. She knocked on Kayla's door.

"Well, hello Madison," Kayla said. "What brings you to grace my office? Don't tell me that you're looking to change the procedural manual. I heard you made quite a stir on the production floor the other day when you went all OSHA on them."

"Well, they needed to be stirred up," Madison replied. "Things were getting rather lax on the floor and people needed to be reminded about the safety regulations."

"Well, I think you have a knack for the job," Kayla replied. "So, what can I do for you?"

"Well, to tell you the truth, I have a school assignment this week regarding insurance, so I decided that this would be a good time to investigate our programs and see what we can do to improve them.

"Well, I would be happy to help," Kayla replied. "I have some ideas if you'd like to let me go over them with you."

"That sounds wonderful," Madison replied.

"Perhaps it wouldn't hurt for you to update your own insurance as they relate to your needs now that you have moved up into administration."

"I guess it can't hurt for us to take a look," Madison said.

For the rest of the day, Madison learned about the company's insurance program from Kayla.

At school, the following day, she discovered that she was going to have to create a project by the following Tuesday where she would have to present the project for a grade. The work project would give Madison a good grade in school and improve the staff health insurance if Seth agreed to the program.

Throughout the rest of the week, Madison and Kayla worked together creating changes that they could make over the next several months to make things better not only for the company but also for the company employees. On Monday she and Kayla, went over the employee insurance plans as they were now. The cost to the employees was more than Madison or the head of HR would have liked and there were more economical options that were just as good. Madison and Kayla then discussed how a health program that encouraged healthy habits could improve coverage to benefit not just the employees, but also the company would have lower overhead costs. They discussed other health options. Kayla was knowledgeable about various programs that could be offered by the company. The education that Madison was experiencing was exciting and she could hardly wait to show the ideas to Seth that she and Kayla wanted to implement.

The insurance program that they chose required that they create a health plan that included lifestyle changes. They would have six months to add an exercise room in the building and provide incentives for maintaining a healthy lifestyle. Following this plan would decrease sick days and help keep the insurance rates low.

"It's the best kind of health plan," Kayla said.

"It's real health care rather than sick care," Madison said to the head of HR. "We just need to design a company gym with weight machines."

"And we can develop exercise routines!" the head of HR replied. "We can put them on YouTube videos and let people use them either in the morning or after work."

"Or even at home if they have to be home for children after work," Madison replied, "and it will save money for the company initially and will save the employees money as their health habits improve."

"We can develop programs that help employees lose weight or help them improve their health habits when dealing with preexisting conditions."

Madison nodded. "If we do that we will have a lot of work ahead of us."

Not only did Madison work on the insurance program for the business, but she also created a PowerPoint presentation to turn in to her teacher for a grade. Kayla helped her with that as well and Madison enjoyed their comradery. Friday they would present the program to Seth and then Madison would use the same PowerPoint presentation for her class the following Tuesday.

They had the entire PowerPoint presentation ready and edited by Friday at noon. Seth said that he would take off the rest of the day on the production floor to check out how they were doing in the office.

Just before lunchtime, Madison went to the catwalk above the production floor to watch the work going on below. There Seth was packing boxes with Rhonda who was laughing a joking with him. She was talking and he was listening and laughing along with her.

Madison felt as though she was stabbed in the heart. *Don't be ridiculous, Madison*, she thought. *He's just your boss.*

Kayla came up to the catwalk.

"Is everything okay?" Kayla asked.

"Oh, yes, I just wanted to see how things are going on the floor," Madison replied. "It seems to be going well."

"Well, I thought I would let you know that there's some pizza and soda and water down at the factory breakroom that Mr. Fisher bought for the entire staff," Kayla said.

"Nice," Madison replied, and she walked with Kayla down to the breakroom. When she arrived, the whistle blew for break time and the employees from the floor came in as well. Seth came in with Rhonda. He touched Darcy's arm as they came into the room where the floor employees had their lunch.

Seth didn't seem to notice Madison who was already in the room with Kayla. He seemed so focused on his conversation with Rhonda.

The green-eyed demon of jealousy rose within Madison. Unable to face this demon at that moment, she took a couple of pieces of pizza and a can of lemon-lime soda and hurried back to her office.

She was taken aback by her reaction to Seth with that girl. Why did she care that he was talking with Darcy and was openly flirting with him? The next thought struck her like a thunderbolt. She had fallen in love all over again with Seth. She set the pizza and soda down on her desk. She then balled her hands into a fist. How could she have let this happen?

She went back to the door to the office and closed it. She leaned her head against it. Her jealousy wasn't only about Ryan's attention to Seth, but Seth's attention to Ryan. She wanted Seth's attention on her, not on Ryan and not on some other woman who worked in their factory. She wanted to be the only woman in Seth's life. That unfortunately was a thing of the past.

She wanted to run away with Ryan and hide. How selfish she suddenly felt, and she tried to shake off the heaviness in the pit of her stomach. She needed to give Seth and Ryan time together. She owed them both that. However, she couldn't help but feel that Seth wanted her as a friend and employee, nothing more.

She sat down at her desk took a bite of the pizza and opened her textbook to see what the next chapter was for her business class. She saw that the subject was the employee payroll system. Payroll was the next subject in her business class so she thought she would get ahead on the subject if Seth didn't have anything else for her to do that day. She ate her pizza while she read. She was deep in her reading when there was a knock on her office door.

"Hey, Madison," it was Seth. He glanced from the soda can and the greasy napkin beside her to the book she was reading. "I was going to let you know there is pizza in the breakroom but see you already got some. I didn't see you in there."

"You were busy," Madison didn't look up from her reading, but she wasn't comprehending any of the reading. Her entire body was tense to Seth's presence in the room, but she didn't want him to know how giddy she was feeling. "Will you be coming by the house to see Ryan tonight?"

"Of course," Seth replied. "Your mother invited me to dinner remember."

"Yeah, I remember," Madison sighed.

"You don't sound like you want me to come," Seth replied.

"No, it's okay," Madison replied. "Ryan would be heartbroken if you didn't come."

Seth cocked his head to the side. "Just Ryan."

Madison smiled. She wasn't about to tell him that she hated every minute that he was out of her sight. Instead, she said, "Well of course, Mom would love to see you too."

"Oh, I see," Seth said.

He did not seem pleased with her answer.

Madison did not know what he meant by 'I see' either.

At that moment, Rhonda came around the corner and stopped in front of Madison's office. "Are you ready to go back to work, Seth?"

Madison didn't miss the use of Seth's first name.

"I'm on my way," Seth replied.

"See you tonight, Madison," he said as he joined Rhonda.

15

∾

Ryan and Seth spent the weekend together. Seth invited Madison to go with them, but she opted to work on her schoolwork rather than spend the weekend at a sporting event with Ryan and Seth. She was able to get ahead with her reading.

When they returned home later that evening, Madison learned that Seth had taken Ryan's friend James with them. Madison wondered how James' mother reacted when the two of them showed up. She imagined that Christine had flirted with Seth in much the same way that the girls at the factory behaved around him. *Not that she should care,* she reminded herself. She had to admit to herself that she was still glad to know that Christine had not gone out with them.

The following Monday Madison and Kayla, the head of the human resources department, presented the insurance program to Seth.

At the end of the presentation, Madison grimaced and said. "Well?"

"You both did a great job on this," Seth said as Kayla turned on the lights after they gave their presentation.

"You should get a good grade in your HR management class, Madison, but I can't use it for the business."

"Why not?"

"The board of directors is not going to go along with the idea of spending more money on employee benefits right now. They told me on my first conference call with them that we need to increase profits because the stockholders are getting a little antsy that the CEO of the business is under thirty years old. We need to prove ourselves. If we don't, they might insist that the business be sold."

"But this idea will save the company money," the Head of HR replied. "We have demonstrated that in our presentation, haven't we?"

"I believe you demonstrated that point out very well. However, like I said, I think it's a great program. I think we will probably be able to implement this program eventually. However, it will cost money right now, and we must prove that we can run this business at a profit. I can tell you what the board of directors is going to say. They are going to ask: 'Who's going to pay for this and that is one aspect of the program, you have not been able to demonstrate."

Can't we talk them into the idea?" Madison asked. "I mean, the employees will be healthier, and they should have fewer sick days. That will save money. Won't it?"

"The theory that having healthier employees will save the company money isn't enough of a reason for the board or the stockholders. Until we demonstrate an increase in productivity and the bottom line, we'll have to put these insurance improvements on hold for now."

"But... "

Seth continued. "Believe me, if it were totally up to me, I would implement it tomorrow. However, if we're going to take care of our employees, we must make sure that they continue to have jobs to come to every day. We must keep up our bottom line or we won't be able to stay in business. Remember that the foundation of being in business is making money."

"I understand that, but. . ." Madison started.

"And I'm telling you, as your proposal stands now, the board will turn it down. Please, Madison, just let it go for now. Turn in your school project for that A and shelf that proposal for now. It's a good plan but. . ."

"But the employees. . ." Madison started.

"Their improved health plan will have to wait. Look, I appreciate all the work you have put into this, and I'm willing to back you when it's time, but for now, we'll have to shelf it. What we need to work on right now is how we can improve production and sales."

For now, Seth was on his own when it came to marketing and sales.

Madison's introduction to marketing and sales class wasn't until the following semester.

Throughout the rest of the week, Seth and Madison went over the notes that Seth took when he was working through the plant. One production machine was obsolete and needed to be replaced. It was the one that Madison had fixed the day that Ryan had arrived, and that he wanted to replace it.

"That machine is quite a bottleneck in our ability to produce our springs," he said. "I think that it's time that we take up the idea that we need to replace this machine with the board of directors. I need to create a PowerPoint presentation so I can demonstrate to the board how much we need to replace this machine right away. I need you to get the specs from the company that makes the replacement machine. Then I need you to crunch the numbers as it relates to the time loss that the machine has caused for the business. Finally, I need you to crunch the numbers to demonstrate how much time would be saved with the new machine and how that converts to dollars saved."

But I'm just a business student!" Madison exclaimed.

"No, you're more than that. You are my assistant," Seth replied, "You're doing quite the job because you know this company as well as anyone. You can do this."

Two days later Madison had the numbers on Seth's desk.

"Perfect, I told you that you could do it!" he said as he looked it over. "I'm going to take this information that you have here and add it to the PowerPoint I created. I'll present it to the board on Friday morning."

Friday morning came, and Seth went to the meeting with the board. Madison was left to work on the paper that she had due the following Tuesday. Seth seemed to take longer than she thought it should take to talk with the board. She hoped that nothing was wrong. She looked at her phone and wondered if she should call him. Had something happened?

When he came back a little after noon, Seth burst into Madison's office.

"I did it!" He exclaimed. "We did it! They agreed to allocate the money for the machine! If it goes as well as you and I think, they'll allow us more money for more flexibility to run the company. I couldn't have done it without you!"

"If I knew all this, I would have expected more of a raise," Madison smiled.

"Well, I can't get you a raise, but I think that you and I should go out to celebrate," Seth exclaimed.

"Should I call Mom and have her get Ryan ready?" Madison asked.

"I think we can leave him home this time. This will be a business dinner of sorts. I'll just have to let Ryan know that he will have me all the weekend," Seth replied. "Dress up in your nicest outfit because I'm taking you to the best restaurant in town!"

Seth followed Madison to the house that evening so he could see Ryan before taking Madison out to dinner.

"Hey Dad!" Ryan exclaimed as Seth drove up behind Madison's car in the driveway.

"Hey son," Seth ruffled the boy's hair as he got out of the Ferrari.

"Can we shoot hoops again tonight?" Ryan asked.

"No, sorry, son, "I have plans for dinner with your mom tonight."

Ryan's expression went from disappointment to excitement. "You mean like a date night?"

Some of Ryan's friends had told him about his parents' date nights. Other friends with single parents or divorced parents probably knew too well about dating. Madison wondered what kids thought about their parents' marital statuses.

Seth ruffled his son's hair again. "Something like that." He then turned his attention toward Madison. "I'll be picking you up at six, okay?

Madison nodded and waved a hand to him as she went into the house.

She knew that she wouldn't have time to shower before going out to dinner, but she knew that she wanted to look the best that she could. She looked at her disheveled hair. She took some dry shampoo and fluffed it up. It was still a little messy, but she would deal with that later. Right now, she needed to decide what to wear.

Madison didn't have many clothes fit to wear to a fancy restaurant, but she did have one dress that would do. It was the simple black dress that she wore to his father's funeral, but she knew that the little black dress could be dressed up with a little jewelry. She had a silver necklace that her parents had bought her the Christmas before her father died. She had never worn it before because her father died before she got a chance, but she would wear it now. In addition, she had a pair of silver-toned earrings that she had picked up that weekend while they had been shopping for Ryan. To finish off the outfit she also wore the black heels that she had worn at her own father's funeral. She then added a white lace shawl that she often wore when she went to church.

Once she was dressed, she touched up her makeup and decided to curl her hair. It wasn't something that she usually did, but she decided that she would this time. She didn't want to embarrass Seth by looking dowdy at a fancy restaurant.

After she finished touching up her hair and makeup, she looked at herself in the mirror. The extra eye makeup and the darker lip color reminded her of how she looked when Seth took her to the prom, not that this was anything like that. She just hoped that he would see her as a woman not just as an employee or as Ryan's mother.

As she came down the stairs, Seth stood at the door with Ryan. Madison couldn't help noticing the way that Seth's eyes lit up when he saw her.

"Wow, Mom, you look like a princess," Ryan exclaimed.

"Yes, she does, doesn't she," Seth turned and ruffled Ryan's head.

"I should take you out for business dinners more often," Seth said as they walked toward the car. Madison cringed. What he said burst the bubble of her dreamy thoughts. This was after all just a business dinner.

Seth held the passenger door of his Ferrari open for Madison and closed it after she settled into the seat.

"So, where are we going?" Madison asked as the powerful engine of the car roared to life.

"I thought you might like Reggie's."

"I've never been," Madison replied.

"Really? "Seth put the car into gear. "I think you'll love it."

Reggie's was a high-end restaurant just outside the country club.

"You have a reservation?" Madison asked. She had heard that it took weeks to get reservations at this place.

"Of course, I do," Seth replied. "I inherited from my father's standing reservation for every Friday night."

Over the past few weeks, he had spent Friday nights with Ryan at his grandmother's house, so he hadn't been here in a few weeks. She wondered if he still had to pay for the night if he didn't come, but of course, it wouldn't be polite to ask.

The parking lot of Reggie's was full of expensive cars of all types. Madison had not realized until that moment how many wealthy people there were in the town who could afford to eat at these kinds of places.

They entered the restaurant, and an employee held the door for them. Seth went up to the host at the entrance.

"Well, hello, Mr. Fisher," the host at the door said. He was dressed in a tux with tails. "Would you like your usual seat?"

"Yes please," Seth replied.

The lights were dimmed as the host led them to a corner of the restaurant where a low light chandelier illuminated a white linen-covered table set with linen napkins, and what looked like genuine silver cutlery along with two crystal goblets at each place setting. In the center of the table were tall white candles on silver candlesticks. The host held out the chair for Madison to sit down and pushed in the chair for her. He then lit the candles that were on the table.

The host left tan menus made of real leather with them.

"What would you like to drink?" Seth asked.

"Some red wine?" she replied.

Seth nodded. "Is there any specific vintage you'd like?"

The only vintage that Madison had ever been able to afford came out of a box. "You choose."

Seth motioned for the waiter, and he came to the table and Seth told him the wine vintage. The waiter was gone for a few minutes and brought the wine. He popped the bottle's cork and allowed Seth and Madison to savor the aroma of the bloom of the wine before pouring it into the glasses.

"Let's do a toast to our first big win as a team against the board," Madison exclaimed.

"Yes," Seth said and raised his glass. Madison did the same. "To our second big win as a team!"

"Second?" Madison asked.

"Yes. I would say that Ryan was our first big win," Seth replied.

Madison blushed. "Of course."

They clinked their glasses together.

"Now that we've toasted our big win, what would you like to order to eat?" Seth asked.

"Oh, I don't know. What would you recommend?"

"You look like a Filet Magnon girl. I think I'd recommend that to you. How does that sound?"

"That sounds good."

"Medium rare?"

"Of course," Madison replied.

Seth then suggested certain other dishes for the other courses and Madison, not knowing some of what he suggested, agreed to his recommendations.

As they ate the soup that was the first course of the meal, Madison said, "Since this is supposed to be a business dinner, I guess we should talk about business. I'm thinking that once we get the production side of things up to par, we'll need to deal with increasing sales so that we don't have products sitting in the warehouse, and we need to assess the raw materials and supplies that we use,"

"You sound like you enjoy your work," Seth replied.

"I do". Madison replied. "I love the fact that I am part of a team that cares about all the employees and helps everyone to make an honest living wage," Madison replied. "I had always said that if I were to get into a leadership position in this or any company, I would consider the needs of the employees as a priority. That's my goal at least."

"Hmm, mine too," Seth replied. "It's good to know that at work we are both on the same page," Seth replied.

Did that mean that he was warning her that in their personal life, they weren't?

While they ate their soup and then through the main course they talked more about business. Seth and Madison talked about various things that they would like to improve in the company and discussed how they could improve both the profits and human relations of the company.

After the main course was cleared from the table, Seth looked down at his drink as if looking for the right words. Madison was suddenly afraid of what he might say. "

"I don't know how else to say this except to blurt it out. I think it would be best if Ryan were to have my last name," Seth said.

"Okay, that sounds like a reasonable request," Madison nodded. "I think Ryan would like that too."

"Good, that was easy enough. Now I have a surprise for you. I know we're not supposed to mix business with pleasure, but... "

"It's your rule," Madison said.

"Yes, it is, but while I was out of the office, I set up a special surprise for you."

"Really?" Madison asked.

"Yes, Seth replied.

"We need to go if we're going to meet our appointment on time."

"Where are we going?"

"Like I said, it's a surprise."

He paid for the meal and the two of them returned to his car. The sun had set behind the hills and Seth drove down along the river as he had when he had taken her home after her car broke down.

It was on the same road as the old house that Madison had always admired and wished she could afford. The old house came into view. Usually, it was dark but this time every light appeared to be on in the house. Seth turned the Ferrari into the driveway behind another car. The car had a placard on the side that said. "Ragnar Real Estate Company".

Madison looked at Seth questioningly. 'What are we doing here?

He said, "While I was out today, I contacted the real estate company that listed the house. I thought it would be fun to bring you to see it from the inside. I called the realtor who listed the house and asked them to let us have a look at the house tonight. Tonight's your chance to dream about what you would like to do with the house if you had it for yourself."

Madison shrugged. *She wondered if perhaps this wasn't such a great surprise after all. She had heard about this technique used to encourage individuals to look at what could be available to them beyond their current situation. Madison wasn't so sure that was true. Seeing the house would probably make her more discontented with her current situation.* "Okay."

A beautiful female real estate agent met them at the door. Her flowing blonde hair was flawless. Her cleavage showed through the opening turned-down collar of her suit. Her skirt is shorter than Madison's dress.

"Good to see you again, Seth," the real estate agent smiled at Seth. The psaltery voice and the familiarity of this voluptuous woman made Madison cringe. The woman was beyond gorgeous. *What man wouldn't find her beautiful and want to date her?* Madison wondered if Seth would call this woman after he dropped Madison off from visiting the house.

She put out her hand to Madison. "Hi, I'm Amanda Forest. You must be Madison. Seth tells me that you would like me to show you around. As you'll see, it needs some work, but it has good bones."

"You'll be in good hands with Amanda, Madison," Seth said. "She showed me around the house this afternoon before I came back to the office. Like she said, It does need a lot of work, but I found it very impressive."

Madison looked from Amanda Forest to Seth. She continued to wonder what the relationship between Seth and Amanda was. Could it be that they were in a relationship? Madison saw Amanda look Seth up and down when Amanda didn't think anyone was looking, but Madison was acutely aware of the other woman's actions. Madison could see that Amanda probably wished it could be so.

"Let me show you around." Amanda's smile at Madison was not as bright as the one she had given Seth.

Amanda opened the front door which led into a great greeting hall. A large chandelier hung down into the room and a grand staircase headed towards the upper floor.

"This stairway leads to the front bedrooms in the house which I will show you in a little bit. The wood on this grand staircase is mahogany and the stairway itself is red oak."

Madison touched the grand staircase banister and looked down at the carpet. The carpet was an ugly shag reminiscent of the 1960s. "This banister is beautiful. You're right, the carpet is ugly. I would rip out all of this throughout the house and if there's hardwood floors under it, I would refinish them."

"Good call. I believe you're right in believing that there are hardwood floors under this carpet," Amanda replied. She pulled up the corner of the carpet where the carpet had already separated from the stretcher.

She looked up at Madison. "See, there is hardwood under this entryway carpet. Shall we check out the great room?"

"Definitely," Madison replied.

"This way," Amanda led her into the grand front room.

Amanda then led them into the front living room.

"How would you change this room," Seth asked. He stood with his pen poised over his notepad.

Amanda pointed out the obvious. "Check out this fireplace. It was built of solid rock right from the grounds the house sits on. The mantel was painted white. "This would be a great place to have parties."

Like I would have fancy parties, Madison thought.

"What would you do here?" Seth asked.

"The first thing I would do is give a good cleaning," Madison ran her finger over the dusty wooden mantel.

"Again, I'd remove the carpet and do hardwood floors and I'd take that paint off that antique mantle and refinish the wood in natural tones. Do you know what the natural wood is?" she asked Amanda.

"I believe that the mantel is the same mahogany that is in the staircase banister.

"So, you'd bring it back to its former glory?"

"Exactly." Madison nodded.

Room after room Amanda asked Madison how she would fix up the house and Madison told her what she thought. Seth wrote down whatever Madison said.

There was a large double door that divided the front room from the back rooms. The rooms in the back included the kitchen, a pantry, and a family room area.

"I think the way that this house is set up, this back part of the house could be used for a family and the front section could be more of a public space."

"You would do that?" Seth asked. "Are you still thinking that this would make a good bed and breakfast?"

"More than ever. It would be easy to set up."

"You could also use the front large living room for big parties and the like," Seth suggested.

"Yeah, as if I would ever be in the position to have large parties," Madison grimaced.

"You never know," Seth said.

"I think you both might be onto something," Amanda replied. "Check out these stairs to the back of the house that goes upstairs."

Amanda led them to a door and opened it to reveal a back stairway that led upward. They were much plainer than the stairway at the front of the house and were enclosed behind the door. The three of them climbed the stairs that led to a hallway. The first room they saw was a large bedroom in which two smaller rooms were connected.

"Seth and I thought that this would be a good location for a master bedroom, Madison," Amanda said. "One of the two rooms could be used as a bathroom and the other as a walk-in closet."

"It could also be used as a nursery," Madison replied. Madison noticed the shocked look on Seth's face and suddenly regretted her statement. Why had she said that? Well, that was what it would have been in her perfect world.

"You would want more children?" Seth asked.

Madison blushed. She had not thought about having other children for a long time. "I don't know. I might if the situation was right," The only man she would consider having children with was Seth, but she knew that he was off-limits. He didn't love her, he was only in her life socially now because of Ryan. He was also her boss.

Madison couldn't see outside the floor-to-ceiling window of the bedroom, but she imagined that it probably overlooked the backyard and the grounds beyond it. The window frame matched the crown molding that circled the room both at the top of the room and around the baseboards. Wainscoting followed the wall where the window was as well as along the solid wall with no doors beside it. The other two walls had doors. On one side was the door that led to the hallway and on the other were two doors to the two other, smaller rooms.

"This room is very ornate. I think that it would be beautiful if it were painted antique white and then antiqued."

Seth was feverishly writing in his notebook.

"What have you been writing?" Madison asked.

"I've just been writing your dream," Seth replied. "If you were to have this house, which room would you choose for Ryan?"

The room across the hall from the master bedroom"

"Why is that?" Seth asked.

"He's going to be a teenager soon enough and I would want him close to the master bedroom." Madison shook her head.

Seth chuckled. "I get that."

"The room is a pretty good size," Amanda said.

"What about the rest of the bedrooms? Didn't you say that there are five others?" Seth asked Amanda.

"That's right," Amanda replied.

Madison continued. "I would fix them up and start a bed and breakfast and give them access to the front stairs and not the back stairs because I would need to be able to keep the house."

"You'd quit your job?" Seth asked.

"Of course not. I get good benefits," Madison replied. She didn't want him to know that she had no desire to quit her job now that she was working with him. "I guess I'd have to get someone to help manage the bed and breakfast. Perhaps Mom would want an additional income too.

Not that I am likely to ever get that chance. I am sure that I will never get that chance."

"What would you do with the outside of the house?" Seth seemed to ignore what she said.

Madison frowned. Why did he stay on this train of thought? She shrugged. She rather enjoyed this road in her imagination. "The grounds would have to be renovated too, of course. It's overgrown, I guess I would get rid of the weeds and provide a yard for Ryan to play with his friends."

At the end of the tour, Seth gave Amanda Forest a nod.

"Alright," she said and went to her car. Discretely, she put a sold sign on the for-sale sign. She then took the sign to her car and placed it in her trunk. She then turned her car around in the driveway and drove away.

"What's going on?" Madison asked.

Seth was smiling. "I bought it for you."

"I don't understand."

"I knew you loved this house, so I purchased it for you. I will do everything you want in this house under one condition."

Ryan looked up from the notebook he was writing in and looked at Madison eye to eye.

"I've enjoyed the time I have spent with Ryan. As you indicated, he's getting older, and you said yourself he needs a father now at this age more than anything. I want to share your dream for this house, but. I want to have custody of Ryan. I want him to live with me."

16

❧

"No!" Madison exclaimed. "I will not trade my son so I can own this house."

"That's not what I am suggesting. Of course not. I would not expect you to. That's not what I want either," Seth said. "I have a better idea that I think would work best for all of us."

"Really? What do you have in mind?" Madison asked.

"I don't want to lose you, Madison any more than I want to lose Ryan. He wants to spend more time with me, and he may not realize it, but he still needs you too. Furthermore, I need you to keep doing what you're doing for business. There are a lot of people dependent on us to keep the business running."

"Well, I'm glad you think that I'm doing a good job, but I don't understand how that has anything to do with Ryan."

"the employees at the factory are a big reason for me to this offer, but so is Ryan's well-being. I want Ryan to have full access to both of us. I remember when I was a kid and my parents were divorced, I used to take advantage of the fact that they didn't get along. I played one against the other, and I don't want to put Ryan in that kind of position."

Madison knew that Seth's parents had divorced when he was just ten years old. He had told her numerous times about the times that he played his father against his mother and his mother against his father. He realized that what he had done was not good for him either.

"That's why I want to share custody of Ryan with you."

"I'm okay with that," Madison replied. "A lot of people share custody of their children. Not all of them are good friends like we are."

"I am relieved that you see me as a friend., and I also want to keep working with you."

"But why give me the house?"

"I wouldn't exactly be giving you the house," Seth replied.

"What are you trying to say?" Madison said. At first, she felt excited. *Could it be that Seth loved her too?*

What he said next quashed that idea.

"You're good for business. I want us to parent Ryan together."

Of course, I have no problem with sharing Ryan's parenting with you. That's it.

It suddenly became clear to Madison that Seth couldn't be in love with her. He was looking for a platonic relationship with her because it was convenient for him. He wanted to share the house with her because of Ryan and the business. *It wasn't because he loved her.* She thought bitterly.

He said something else, but she was so deep in her thoughts that she missed what he said.

"I'm sorry. What did you say," she asked.

"I said, I think that we should get married for Ryan's sake. I'm asking you to marry me."

"I... I don't know what to say," she murmured.

She was in shock. What could she say? She wanted nothing more than for him to ask her to marry him, but this was not the marriage proposal that she had always dreamed of. This wasn't about love, well, not about love for her anyway. It was about his love for his son. She didn't want to marry him like this. *Not like this,* she thought as Seth continued to speak.

"If we are married, we can give Ryan the best advantage. Your parents stayed together, and I admired them for that. You and I work well together. I want the same for Ryan as I know that you do. I don't want it to be like my parents who divorced when I was nine. Please, marry me because of Ryan."

"I don't know," Madison replied. She suddenly had another thought. Could it be that he was trying to manipulate her because of the company?

"So, you'd be taking money from the business to buy the house?" She was grabbing at straws to keep from thinking about answering the marriage question. "I don't want to take money from the business for the house."

Madison realized as soon as she said it, where the money came from for the house was none of her business.

Seth didn't seem to begrudge her interest in his financial affairs. "No, I have some money of my own from selling my house in Europe and shares in the business in Europe. I'll also be selling my father's house. I can afford the house, Madison, even if you can't."

"Alright. I see. Of course, I will do it for Ryan and the business. Yes, I'll do it."

He had said nothing about being in love with her, so she couldn't tell him that she loved him. He was marrying her not because he loved her but because he wanted things to be right for Ryan and for the people at the business. She would do it. Seth said that he needed her, and she knew that he loved Ryan. That was better than nothing. She hoped that perhaps he would one day love her too. It wouldn't happen if she refused him now.

"It's settled then," Seth replied. "We will pick up the engagement ring tomorrow."

"When will this marriage take place?" Madison asked. *This was not the kind of marriage proposal that she had always dreamed of having from Seth, but she guessed it would have to do. This was more of a business proposition than it was a marriage proposal, but she would have to take it even if it was all she would ever get. At least Ryan would be happy with this turn of events. What was she thinking? He would be ecstatic.*

"Well then, it's settled. I want us to be married as soon as possible, but I want us to be able to move into this house when we do. I don't want us living at your mother's house, and I don't want us moving into my father's house either. As I see it, your plan makes it possible to fix up the kitchen, the master bedroom, and Ryan's room so that we could live in just those rooms before the wedding and then deal with the rest of the house after moving in. If we can find a contractor to handle the remodeling right away, I think we can get the house done within a couple of months. That should give us enough time to get the house livable and to prepare for our wedding."

Madison nodded. *Why did she feel let down? She was getting what she always wanted, wasn't she? Perhaps it was because reality didn't match up to what she had fantasized about what life with Seth would be like. Well, she wasn't in high school anymore and she was too old for fairytales.*

Seth seemed to have thought it all out. Seth then began planning for the next two months. A lot of those plans fell on Madison. She would not only need to do her studies and learn her job at the factory, but she also had to make plans for the wedding and implement plans for the house with contractors and designers to get the house ready for occupancy by the wedding day.

She loved Seth, but she knew she couldn't make him love her. He was giving her everything that she ever wanted except the one thing that she wanted and that was Seth's love for *her*. Yes, he loved Ryan, and she was grateful for that, but she wanted more than that from him. She wanted him to love *her* too. She decided to just be grateful for what she was given.

After that, Seth took her home. He followed her up onto the porch. It was dark outside, and the porch light was on.

"This reminds me of when we were teenagers," Seth said. He was standing face-to-face with her. She looked up into his eyes. As usual, they were kind, but there was no passion in them. "I think we have an audience."

He motioned to the window where out of the corner of her left eye she saw that Ryan was watching them from behind the curtain in the window.

"Let's give him something to get excited about," Seth replied. At first, Madison didn't know what to think, but then she realized his intentions when he pulled her close bent over, and kissed her on the mouth. Madison savored the moment when he touched his lips to hers. She wanted more. She hoped that the kiss would deepen, but though the kiss lingered, Seth didn't take it further than the touching of their lips.

She wanted more. What would he do if she kissed him back in the way that she wanted?

But. . .she sighed and stepped back.

"Good night, Seth," she said quietly. "We'll see you in the morning then?"

This time it was Seth who seemed confused, but he quickly recovered. "Yes, I think Ryan will be ecstatic and get a kick out of helping us pick out the ring. Don't you think?"

"Yes, he will," Madison said softly. "I'll see you in the morning."

With that, she unlocked the door and slipped inside.

Once inside Ryan rushed Madison and gave her a big hug. "Did you and Dad have fun tonight?"

Ryan had already bathed and was dressed in a pair of his new sports pajamas.

"Of course," Madison replied. *What else could you tell a seven-year-old? How could you tell your son that you're walking into a sham of a marriage for his sake?* "We have a surprise to share with you tomorrow, Ryan. To tell you the truth, your dad and I have a couple of them."

"What is it? What is it? What is it?" He asked. "Does it have anything to do with the kiss he gave you on the porch?"

She had to hand it to Ryan for being good at putting two and two together.

Madison tilted her head from side to side. "Maybe. We'll have to wait until tomorrow when your dad is here to find out the answer to that question. How about we get you to bed now so tomorrow can come faster," Madison took her son's hand and led him up the stairs to his room.

In the morning, Madison awoke to Ryan shaking her on the shoulder.

"It's morning Mom!" Ryan exclaimed. He was already dressed in his favorite sports sweatshirt, jeans, and school athletic shoes. "Time to get up."

Madison moaned and looked at the clock on her phone. It was only five-thirty. "No, it isn't. The stores won't be open for hours. How about you go watch a movie until it's time to go."

Ryan sulked out of the room. "I can't wait!"

Madison shook her head and pulled the blanket over her head. A few minutes later, Ryan returned. "I'm bored."

Madison moaned and looked at the time on her phone. Less than half an hour had passed since he had been in the room.

Madison moaned again and threw back the covers. "Alright, I'll get up. Are you ready for breakfast?"

Madison was pouring a bowl of breakfast cereal for Ryan when Seth arrived.

"Do you have a bowl for me?" he asked.

"Sure," Madison replied and took another bowl out of the cupboard and put it in front of Seth. "I hope you don't mind eating what Ryan is eating. It's the only cereal we have. Mom and I usually just have coffee and toast. Would you like some coffee?"

"Yes, please," he said.

As they sat down at the table, Diane came into the room. "Well, you all are certainly here early today, Seth. What have you all got planned today?"

"You mean to say that you haven't told them yet?" Seth looked at Madison accusingly.

"I thought we would tell them together," Madison replied.

Seth got up from his chair at the breakfast table and stood behind Madison's chair. He put his hands on her shoulders. She raised her hand and put it on Seth's hand on the same shoulder.

"Madison has agreed to marry me," Seth squeezed her shoulders slightly.

Ryan's squeal of delight drowned out Diane's gasp.

Madison reached back and touched Seth's hand on her shoulder. "We've also purchased an old house on the river,"

"What house is that?" Diane asked.

Madison told her.

"Are you serious? Do you know what fixing that place up will cost?"

"I have someone coming out Monday to give an estimate of what the job entails. Madison has some great ideas for the house. It will be a great investment."

"You should see it inside, Mom. The house has potential."

"I'm sure it does. You'll both have to show me around the house," Diane replied.

"Soon, Mom," Madison said. "Soon."

The three of them again took Madison's car, and again, Madison drove. Seth directed Madison to drive to Mayer's Jewelry Store.

"Are you sure you don't want to go to Discount Jewelry," Madison asked. "The prices are a lot more reasonable."

Seth waved her off. "Don't be ridiculous. Nothing's too good for my girl."

Hearing him say that she was his girl made her heart leap, but reality struck her like a freight train that he was saying it for Ryan's benefit when he said. "Isn't that right, buddy?"

'Yeah!" he exclaimed.

"You're going to help us pick out the perfect one for your mother too. Aren't you?"

"Yeah!" he said with equal enthusiasm.

Madison would have been happy with a simple gold band and no engagement ring, but Seth immediately went to the case with the most expensive rings. Ryan pointed at a big flashy wide gold band with a square-cut garnet setting.

"You could wear one like that," Ryan said.

"No son, those are men's rings," Seth replied. He directed his son toward the more delicate-looking women's rings.

Madison decided to go along with Ryan's idea. "Sure Seth, it would make you a great wedding ring."

Seth thought for a minute and then said. "Yeah, I think you're right. This can be my wedding band. Now, let's find you the perfect bridal set."

At that moment the jewelry store attendant came up to the counter. "Have you found what you are looking for?"

"We found part of what we want," Madison replied. "Can my fiancé try on the garnet ring there?"

Madison felt a twinge of anxiety when she used the term "fiancé", but Seth remained poker-faced, so Madison wasn't sure how he felt about her use of the word.

"Certainly," the attendant exclaimed. She took the ring from the case and Seth tried it on.

"What do you think, Madison," he asked as they all admired the ring.

"I think that it is perfect," Madison replied. She liked looking at his hand and the ring did look good on it.

"We'll take it," Seth exclaimed.

The ring didn't need any resizing.

"Would you like to take it with you today?" the attendant asked.

'Yes, that would be fine," Seth replied then asked. "What do you like, Madison?"

Madison went over to a case where there was a simple white gold band and an engagement ring with a small diamond chip.

"No, that will never do for my girl," Seth replied. "How about this one?"

He picked out a set of the same white gold. Instead of the simple diamond chip, there was a three-carat diamond in the engagement ring and several small diamonds in the wedding band. "Now this is more what I have in mind."

That's a little too much for me," Madison replied. "How about this one."

She picked out another set with a plain band and a smaller diamond solitaire on the engagement ring.

"No, that will never do," Seth replied, and the attendant helped them choose the ring set.

The ring set that they chose was bathed in the opulence of a gleaming antique gold solitaire engagement ring with a setting that featured intricate floral detailing on both the inside and outside of the band for added luxury. A classic prong setting was secured in a two-carat round center solitaire diamond.

The ring was sized for Madison and the plan was to pick up the sized ring in a few days.

"That didn't take long. What do you want to do now, Ryan?" Seth asked the boy.

"Can we see the new house?"

"I was hoping you'd say that, Sport," Seth replied. "Let's go check out the house. Your mom hasn't seen the grounds yet."

"I saw it years ago," Madison interjected.

Okay, correction acknowledged. Your mom hasn't seen the house in years," Seth ruffled his son's hair. "While we look things over, we'll decide where we want your basketball court!"

"All right!" Ryan exclaimed.

They stopped by the house. Already someone had mowed most of the yard. Someone was weed-eating the grass in the front yard.

"I hope you don't mind, but I called a mowing company to get started on the yard," Seth replied. "I wanted to start getting a handle on this place, so I had a lawncare company start clearing out around the house."

Madison felt slighted that he took control of getting the house and then starting with the exterior without her even getting a chance to look over the property. *She would have liked to have seen it in its wild state. She wanted to see what flowers were already planted around the property, but that would not be something that she could do now because Seth had already taken the initiative to rip out the yard.*

Madison wouldn't ask Seth about that right now. She didn't want to confront him in front of Ryan. She would have the chance to do that later when the boy wasn't in earshot.

Before going into the house, Seth took Ryan into the backyard. "Now Sport, what do you think?"

"It's a big yard," he said and began looking around. "Wow, is that a pool?"

"Well, yes, it was," Seth replied. He then turned toward Madison. "Do you think we could fix the pool?"

"If that's what you want!" Madison shrugged.

Seth shrugged and turned to Ryan. "Well, Sport, how about your mom and I show you the inside of the house!"

"Yeah," Ryan exclaimed. He ran toward the house. He tried to open the door.

"It's not opening!" He called back to his father.

"I'm sorry, Ryan, I have to unlock the door for you," Seth stepped in front of his son and took the keys out of his pocket. He put the key into the door, turned it, and opened the door wide.

"This way, young sir," he made a gallant wave on his hand toward the house.

"Open that door," Seth said when they got to the door to the back stairway. Seth showed Ryan the back stairway and led him up to the bedroom across from Madison and Seth's room.

"This is it? It stinks in here!" Ryan exclaimed as he went into the room.

Old mildew-smelling carpeting of the same green shag carpeting covered the floor, and dingy walls and ceiling needed a coat of paint.

"The carpet is old and . . ."

"It will be a lot different when we get your room redecorated. We'll take out the carpet and repaint the walls and ceiling, and we'll fix it for you exactly how you want it."

'Okay," Ryan said, but he didn't sound very convinced.

"You just wait," Seth said. "We'll not only make this your sports room, but You'll have your own television and your own computer. You'll be able to play video games here with your friends."

"All right!" Ryan punched the air. "When can we start taking out the carpet."

"I'm not sure, but we do have someone coming on Monday to tell us when that can happen."

"Can I help take out the carpet?" Ryan asked.

"Sure, Sport," Seth said. "Guess what I have for this afternoon, Ryan?" Seth asked.

'What?" Ryan asked.

"Well, since you were such a good sport about this morning, I thought that this afternoon you and I could go to a college football game at the local college," Seth then turned to Madison. "I hope you don't mind if I just take Ryan, do you?"

Madison shook her head. "Of course not. I don't mind at all. I have some schoolwork to finish this afternoon."

She said that, but she did care. Seth had told Ryan that he had tickets to a football game and then in front of Ryan, he asked Madison if it was all right. Madison didn't appreciate being played that way.

Seth clenched his fist and tapped the air. "Great! How about if we go as a family out to Applebee's for dinner tonight after the game? We'll bring your mom along with us."

"I'm sure she'd like to take a break from cooking dinner," Madison replied.

They all rode back to Madison's mother's house where Seth and Ryan exchanged Madison's car for Seth's Ferrari."

Madison went up to her room, took her laptop out with her to the patio, and sat down in a chai tea. She pulled it up to the table that overlooked the backyard.

The weather for that time of the year was nice. There was a breeze from the south which indicated that the warm weather would continue at least for the next day or so.

Madison spent the next hour doing her reading assignment when her mother came out to the patio with two cups of coffee in hand. She handed one to Madison who took a sip.

"This is exactly what I need right now, thanks, Mom."

"For someone who just got engaged," Diane said. "You don't look very happy."

"I..." Madison felt hot tears at the corners of her eyes. She shook her head.

"What's wrong? You do love Seth. Don't you?" Diane asked.

"Of course, I do."

"I hear a but coming," Diane knew her daughter very well and Madison knew that she wasn't going to be able to keep up the play-acting with her mother.

"I love him, but I don't know that he loves me," Madison blurted out.

"Of course, he loves you. Why would he do everything that he's doing if he didn't love you?" Diane asked.

"Because of Ryan," Madison replied. "He's marrying me because his parents divorced when he was a young boy, and he doesn't want that kind of life for his son."

"Are you sure? Did he tell you that?" Diane asked.

"Well, not in so many words, but he as good as told me that!"

"Hasn't he told you that he loved you?"

Madison shook her head.

"And you're okay with this?"

"Of course not, but what choice do I have?"

"If you're not sure whether he loves you or not, I think you need to ask him point blank how he feels about you. You should clear the air. The two of you must communicate your true feelings."

"I can't ask him point blank. What if he says that. . .."

"Why? Because you're afraid of what he might say?'

Madison nodded. "I think I would rather not know that he only cares about how our relationship affects Ryan or the job. At least I can be near him that way."

"The job?"

Madison nodded again. "Yes. He says I'm good for business too."

"I think you're wrong about him not loving you. He's given you the position that he gave you at the plant. You're a coward, Madison. You are acting like a coward, and I didn't raise any coward."

"Not because he cares about me," Madison replied. "It's because he knows I'm good for business."

"Then there's the house," Diane said. "What man gives a woman a house if he just cares for her?" Diane asked.

"He's doing it because it allows him to have access to Ryan and keeps me on the job."

"What's to stop him from using his money to just take you to court to get custody of Ryan."

"He wants Ryan to have two parents married to each other. He also thinks that I am important to the business."

"Oh, I'm sure that having you know the business as well as you do is convenient for him, but I'm sure that he could find people who know as much or more than you do about the spring business. What you're suggesting sounds more like Harrison Fisher than it does like Seth Fisher. I think you're underestimating the young man."

Madison shook her head. Diane had been quick to forgive and forget Seth's indiscretions. She had always been fond of Seth, and Madison doubted that her mother would ever think poorly of Seth.

"I went down that road once and he broke my heart," Madison said.

"You can't blame Seth for his father's manipulations!"

"And there's still the fact that Seth married another woman, Mom!" Madison replied. "He hadn't talked to me since that day that he left and then not long afterward, he ended up married."

"Well, it's obvious that he's no longer married to that woman. Perhaps it's time you forgave him and moved on with your life. If you continue to hold that against him, you might just find yourself alone again. Take charge of the things that you can take control of and just enjoy the fact that Seth is back in your life. Trust me, it will all work out."

"I don't know, Mom," Madison started.

"Well, I do. Stop worrying about everything. You're going to get married, and you have a wedding to plan and a house remodel. Make this wedding about you. You are the bride after all. Turn that house into the one that you always knew that it could be. Make it your home. Enjoy the process."

Madison closed her online book and her laptop. She kissed her mother on the forehead and left the patio while Diane continued to enjoy the sunset.

She put her laptop on the desk in her bedroom and decided to take a shower. She allowed the water to pour over her as she thought about her relationship with Seth. She looked down at her left ring finger soon it would have that big diamond on it.

It was all too much for Madison. Somewhere deep inside she felt as though Seth was trying to control her life in the same way that his father controlled her. He was using her for his purposes. She didn't feel that her mother was right about Seth not needing her for the job and could have had any person that he wanted as his assistant but chose her. He was marrying her to keep her from marrying someone else and...

She had to stop this roller coaster of feelings. She could not believe that Seth was only using her for his end. Her mom was probably right. That was Seth's father's way of doing things. Seth was not his father. At least, that was what she hoped.

17

〜

Madison took her mother's words to heart and decided to make the best of the situation and create the wedding that she had always wanted. She wanted a simple wedding. She never wanted a big wedding. She wanted a simple wedding that would only include the immediate family. In the past, she had been a bridesmaid for friends and the days leading up to the weddings had been exhausting. She vowed she would never put herself in that position if she ever got married.

Even though she didn't want a big wedding, she still wanted it to be beautiful. When Seth saw her plans, he wasn't exactly on board.

"Why don't you want a big wedding?" Seth asked. "I thought every bride wanted all the glitz and the glamour?"

"It's just too much work to plan a huge wedding, work with the contractor and the interior designer, go to school, work as your assistant, and be Ryan's mother all in two months is quite enough for me to have on my plate."

"I'd be happy to spend more time with Ryan," Seth replied. "Plus, the wedding is planned for the Saturday between Christmas and New Year. Business will be slowing down after Thanksgiving and your semester ends in the middle of December as well. You're organized. I'm sure you can manage. I have never seen you fail at meeting deadlines. In addition to taking care of Ryan, I can do anything you need me to do."

At work, Seth and Madison said nothing to anyone about their engagement because they did not have Madison's ring yet. However, the following Saturday, they picked up the diamond ring set from the jewelers and before they left the store, Seth put the ring on Madison's finger and kissed the ring.

"Sealed with a kiss," he said and looked up at Madison. She turned away and couldn't meet his gaze. She didn't want him to see how much she loved him.

On Monday morning, Beca the receptionist's face lit up when she saw Madison's ring.

"What a gorgeous ring," Beca said. "I didn't even know that you were dating anyone. Who is the lucky guy?"

As if on cue, Seth arrived in the office as well and saw Madison standing in front of Beca's desk. He went right over to Madison. Madison shuttered as he put his arm around her waist "Good morning, Beca. I see Madison has been showing off her ring."

"You and Madison?" Beca asked.

"Of course, we have decided to pick up where we left off when we were in high school," Seth smiled. "Now, my darling, let's get to work."

Madison followed him toward their offices.

"Why did you tell Beca that?" Madison asked as soon as they were outside Beca's earshot.

"Because this way she will be letting everyone know that we're engaged. It will save us from having to try to explain to everyone else our sudden engagement."

"I guess you're right. You are the boss," Madison replied. *This way they could also stay on task on the job. Plus, they would be telling everyone the same story. Not that it was just a story. In a sense it was true.*

That afternoon, the phone rang. Madison picked up the phone and gave her usual greeting.

"Hello, Ms. Baton, this is Mark Delaney of Delaney Contracting. Mr. Seth Fisher called me to ask me to be the contractor of your house on River Drive. I understand that you want this project to start right away. Since it is fall, my calendar is pretty much clear so I can begin right away."

Seth must have called the contractor that morning because Seth had said nothing to her about finding a contractor to do the work. He had done his part. He had found the contractor, but the actual work of designing and making the house as she wanted it, fell on Madison.

"Oh, yes," Madison didn't know what to say.

When can you meet me at the house to see what you had in mind for the house," the contractor continued. "Can we possibly meet this evening after you get off work?"

"Of course," Madison replied. Since it was Monday, she did not have school that day. They discussed the time and Madison rang off.

At the house, the contractor listened to Madison's ideas. After going through the house and looking over the furnace and other utilities, he gave his verdict on how to proceed.

"I think that since you want to focus on finishing the living area in the back of the house, I think we'll begin there. We'll separate it from the rest of the house so that you can move in without the dust while we finish the front. However, first, we need to get the plumbing, the electricity, and the furnace up to code. I think that we should see if I can get an electrician out here tomorrow or the next day to get this ball rolling."

The electricity and plumbing on the entire house as well as the heating and air conditioning were also updated for the entire house. Most of the back of the house was gutted including the kitchen. However, Madison had insisted that the old cabinets be refurbished and covered with granite countertops.

For a while, the family area of the house looked like a cyclone had hit. After that, progress on the house moved quickly on the rooms in the back, both upstairs and down were separated immediately.

When Madison's classes ended in mid-December, she marveled at the progress that had been made in just six weeks.

In addition to the plumbing of one of the bathrooms upstairs and the kitchen had to be updated A second bathroom had to be added to the master suite. In addition to the bathroom, Madison decided to have a walk-in closet after all. They could later knock out a wall to connect the master suite with a room that they could use for a nursery in the future if they needed it.

In the kitchen, the old kitchen cabinets were refinished, and the granite countertops were installed. A modern deep farm sink replaced the old two-bowl sink. A dishwasher was also added. The stainless-steel refrigerator, ovens, and cooktop were added. A grill was built into the gas cooktop. In a small room off the kitchen was the utility area where the water heater, furnace, and laundry area were located. On the other end of the kitchen was a small breakfast nook with a built-in side cabinet where they kept a microwave, coffee maker, storage space, and small refrigerator so that they could have an easy breakfast. Beyond the breakfast nook was the room to the right of the breakfast nook was to be the formal dining room where there were the doors that led into the rest of the house. This way, if they had a big event, they could open the doors between the dining room and the main part of the house or keep it closed if they just wanted to have a family dinner in the formal dining room.

The dining room was freshly painted, and the floors were sanded and refinished. The room remained unfinished. Seth and Madison decided to wait until they had moved into the house before they purchased the furniture and décor for the room. Beyond the nook area was another room that they would use as their family room.

There were still a few details to complete but the contractor and the designer assured Madison that they would be completed by their wedding day.

Madison had wanted her mother to come live with them right away, but both Diane and Seth said that it would be better if she just stayed in her own house. For now, Diane would continue living in her house and come daily to make sure that Ryan had someone there when he came home on the bus. Fortunately, he did not have to change schools when they moved, but he would have to take a bus to school rather than it being necessary for one of the adults in his life to drive him to school.

The next two weeks seemed to pass even more quickly. To Madison, the days passed like a whirlwind, and she didn't have time to catch a breath, not to mention think about what was happening in her life.

Her responsibilities continued to increase at work and she was preparing for the wedding, and supervising the remaining details of the house kept her constantly busy. Plus, she attended Ryan's holiday school activities with Seth. It only seemed right that they did. To get everything done on time, Madison had to focus on meeting her immediate deadlines if she wanted to make it all work.

The night before the wedding, she was looking over the last of the preparations when suddenly she panicked.

It was as if everything that she could ever ask for was now suddenly coming true, but she still wasn't satisfied. She had the job she wanted. She had the house she wanted, and she was marrying the man of her dreams. The problem was that she was sure that Seth didn't love her as she wanted him to. She had a career that she had always wanted, but she felt as though she had somehow not earned her place in the business. She had the house of her dreams and had the money it would take to finish fixing it up to its modern version of its former grandeur, but she was still uneasy like the shoe was about to drop.

The living areas of the house were ready for occupancy. Seth and Ryan worked directly with the decorator decorating Ryan's bedroom with football-themed decor The master suite was classic in design. It was feminine enough for Madison but masculine enough for Seth. The designer did an awesome job of unifying their tastes into a room where they both felt comfortable. It helped that Seth said that the cost didn't worry him.

The breakfast nook was a simple room with a booth like they have in restaurants and a counter. The small refrigerator was built into the countertop. The refrigerator would be used to hold milk and juice for convenience so that they didn't have to go into the kitchen. There was also a small microwave built into it as well. This way when there were bed and breakfast guests, they wouldn't get in Diane's way as they ate their breakfast before starting their day.

The sitting room, as Seth called the family room, was a cozy room that was furnished with an 82-inch smart television on one wall with a sectional couch that had three reclining chairs built facing it. In the center of the floor in front of the sectional couch was a glass table. Just off the sitting room was a small office for Seth or Madison to work at home if either of them needed to. The office wasn't much more than a closet, but as Seth said. Neither one of them wanted to take away from their family time anyway.

The kitchen would have been any woman's dream kitchen. Black granite countertops, a center island. Rows of cabinets on both sides of the room were built from floor to ceiling, most of which stood empty because Madison had no dishes, pots or pans, or cutlery to fill it. That too would be added over time.

Beautiful but as empty as my soul, she thought. *How long I can live feeling this emptiness?*

All this running around prevented her from feeling and now that she took the time to analyze it, she felt empty. She suddenly was afraid she was losing control of who she was. Things were moving too fast. Not only that, but Seth had never told her that he loved her. Things would be different if he told her that. No, she didn't want him to just tell her. She might be able to get him to say that he loved her if she just asked him to, but she wanted him to tell her that he did and in so many words without being asked. Oh, he acted lovingly toward her. At work all day, they stuck to business and Seth was affectionate, but Madison felt that it was primarily because it was expected of him in public. After work, they would act lovingly toward one another because it was expected of them. When they were around Diane and Ryan, Seth was very attentive. He would throw his arm around her and would kiss her on the forehead. He would lay his hand over her ringed hand when they sat on the couch at Diane's house going over wedding and house plans. The problem was it was all fake. They were never alone together. Ryan seemed to make sure that there was always someone around them so they couldn't be alone.

Madison awoke on the day of the wedding to the sound of thunder. She moaned. She looked out her window and saw the rain spraying against her window. She pulled her pillow over her head and moaned again. She wouldn't be able to stay in bed because there was so much that she had to do.

Was this an omen for her future with Seth?

"Madison, time to get up," Diane called. There was a knock on her door.

"I'm up," she felt like she was a teenager again.

She looked around the room and already it looked bare. The framed photos that had been on her dresser had been packed as were most of her clothes. Ryan's room had been emptied as well. Everything had been taken over to the house on River View Road. All that was left of her things was a suitcase filled with the clothes she would wear before the wedding, her wedding dress, and other things she would need for the day.

She got out of bed and went to the bathroom to shower. As the warm water sprayed over her body, she realized that she would not be showering in this house again. She would not be sleeping in her bed again. She would be Mrs. Seth Fisher. Tonight, she would be spending in the new home that she had always dreamed of owning. Ryan would have his father, but something important was lacking. She could not feel satisfied. She felt so miserable.

By the time she finished her shower, the thunderstorm had ended, and the sun was peeking out from behind the clouds. It was going to be a beautiful day after all.

She dressed in a pair of jeans and a collared, button-down, and front-opening blouse. She carried her plastic-covered wedding dress and hung it on the door. She put her shoes and stockings in a suitcase and put the suitcase beside the hanging dress.

She and her mother then put their wedding clothes that were protected in plastic in the car and went to the salon for a makeover for the wedding.

Ryan had spent the night with Seth at the new house. Seth was planning to take the boy out to breakfast and then would take him to the church. Madison wasn't worried about his clothes for the wedding because Seth had picked them up the day before. The rest of his belongings which had been brought the day before waited in his room to be put away in his new bedroom.

The church was a small chapel that Madison had always thought was a beautiful place to get married and she was surprised that Seth agreed without hesitation that they could be married there. The wedding planner had found the minister who would be officiating the ceremony for them. The wedding planner ensured that the church was decorated, and the flowers were where they needed to be.

Madison decided to wear flowers instead of a veil. Despite the wedding's simplicity, Madison was still nervous that everything would be a disaster. If the wedding planner did not show up, things would have been disastrous.

As Madison and Diane settled into the hairdresser's chairs, the wedding planner brought the fresh white orchids to the hairdresser's salon.

"Thank God you're here," Madison said. "I was afraid you wouldn't make it here on time."

"I would never be late for such an important day," she said. She opened the box that held the orchid and handed it to the hairdresser.

Now that she had joined them though, Madison breathed a sigh of relief. She was glad that she had kept things simple.

"I already put your bouquet in your dressing room at the chapel," the wedding planner said. "Do you remember everything you need to do?"

Madison nodded.

As the hairdresser and the other women at the beauty salon did their magic, Madison thought about the night before. That evening, they went to the chapel for the rehearsal and then afterward, they went to the same restaurant for the rehearsal dinner as Seth and Madison had discussed the idea of getting married in the first place.

Seth had arrived late at the church for the rehearsal. Ryan was with him and there was an older woman as well.

"I have a surprise for you, Madison. I'd like you to meet my mother."

"Your mother?" Madison knew that she was still alive, but Madison didn't realize that Mariya Fisher was going to be at the wedding, but then why wouldn't she attend the wedding of her only son?

Seth introduced her to his mother. She was tall with dark flawless hair and makeup. Her eyes were dark brown. The smile on her face reached her eyes, which was something that Madison had never seen with Seth's father.

"It's so nice to finally meet you. I'm Mariya Grant. I changed my name back to my maiden name after the divorce," Mariya explained and then said. "Seth has told me so much about you."

"Really?" Madison asked. She wondered if Mariya had been to Seth's first wedding. She was sure Mariya must have been to that one as well.

"Of course," Mariya said. "I knew that by the way he always talked about you that. . ."

Before she could finish Seth came up to them. "It's nice to see that the two of you are getting to know each other."

"And I am hurt that you didn't keep me in the loop," Mariya replied. "You should have called me long before you did so I could have helped with the preparations."

"Which is exactly why I didn't call you until we had all our plans made, Mom," Seth replied.

"You could have at least told me I had a grandson!" Mariya replied. "You didn't tell me about Ryan until you picked me up at the airport!"

'It was a nice surprise, wouldn't you say?"

Mariya patted him on the cheek. "You are full of surprises, my son."

Reggie's was the best in the area, and it only seemed right to him that they should go there. Ryan was impressed with the restaurant and was looking forward to telling his friends about it. Madison was happy for her son. Everything was as perfect for him as it could be. He was also impressed with his new grandmother.

Madison learned from Mariya that Seth had arranged for her to use a different full-service beauty salon than Madison to get ready for the wedding.

Madison and Diane had their hair styled, makeup done, and nails done, and Diane drove the two of them to the church. Seth's Ferrari was already in the parking lot, but Diane and Madison went in a different door than Seth used because their dressing room was in a different part of the church so Seth wouldn't see the wedding dress before the wedding.

The dress was not the long and flowing dress that brides typically wore. Madison's dress was mid-length with an uneven hemline. There was a sleeveless silk underdress and an open weave lace overlay that came over the underdress that had tight-fitting sleeves.

"Oh, Madison, you look beautiful," Diane replied. "Your father would have been so proud."

Madison smiled a sad smile. "I miss Daddy."

"Your father would have been so happy for you. I am certain of that," Diane smiled. Madison gave her a peck on the cheek.

"I'm just glad that you're standing up for me. I wouldn't want anyone else to stand up for me."

Madison's mother was not only going to be her bridesmaid, but she was also going to walk her down the aisle and give her away. She wanted to keep the wedding as simple as possible.

Madison and Diane walked from their dressing room to the back of the church. As they walked in front of the glass doors at the back of the church, Madison noticed that the parking lot was full of cars.

"What in the world," Madison looked out the door. "Why are all those cars here."

"You mean you don't know?" Diane asked.

"No," Madison replied.

"Well, Seth invited all of them because he thought you were just too busy to handle inviting the guests."

"Are you kidding me?" Madison asked.

"Now, Madison, you know that Seth was just trying to help out."

"Trying to take control of my life you mean."

"Now, Madison," Diane replied. "Are you going through with this or not?"

As much as she questioned some of Seth's actions. She couldn't imagine not having him in her life. "Yes, let's do this."

Her mother took her daughter by the arm and the two of them started up the aisle.

18

❦

Madison fixed a smile on her face. She looked up toward the front of the small church where Seth was standing. She started recognizing the faces of those who had come to the ceremony. Some were from the factory and on the groom's side of the church she saw Seth's mother dressed in a pink chiffon and lace pants suit.

Diane walked Madison down the aisle and then acted as the matron of honor and Ryan was the best man although, for legal reasons, the pastor would witness the marriage document.

As Seth was kissing Madison at the end of the ceremony, he whispered into her ear. "There's a reception downstairs."

"You've outdone yourself," Madison replied. "Another surprise?"

"I knew you were busy." Seth flashed a smile that Madison knew she could not resist. "I wanted to surprise you."

The two of them walked down the church aisle together as the

Diane and Mariya had joined the newlyweds in the reception line.

As if on cue, Ryan, who started with his parents on the reception line, began to get restless.

"Dad, can I go play with my friends now?" Ryan asked.

Seth nodded. "All right but hug your mom and your grandmothers first."

Ryan grinned. "I got a new Dad and a new grandma!"

Ryan hugged his mother and then went to his Grandma Baton and hugged her as well. He then went to his Grandmother Grant and hugged

130

her. He then put his arms around both of his parents. "I love you, Mom and Dad!"

The happy, energetic Ryan ran off to play with his friend Blaze Fox, the son of one of the people that his parents worked with.

"He seems like such a good boy," Mariya replied.

"He is," Diane, Madison, and Seth all said in unison.

"I have missed so much time with him. Was he this good when he was a baby?"

"He was," Diane replied. "He's been a real joy to have around all of his life."

"I think it was cruel of Harrison to purposely keep the boy a secret. I am still marveling that I am a grandmother. You must be proud of how well Madison has done with him."

Diane nodded. "Madison has done well. I am proud that Madison knew how to be a good mother even though she was so young when she had him."

"I think Harrison may kept have Ryan a secret not only to keep Seth from Madison but also to keep me from knowing that I had a grandson. He knew how much I valued family! I'm glad Seth isn't more like him."

"Mother," Seth said. "Let's not talk about the past. Today's Madison's and my wedding day. Let's celebrate."

The wedding guests had all gone through the reception line and the DJ, whom Seth also hired without Madison's knowledge, had started playing music.

Mariya nodded.

"Shall we show our guests how well we dance together?" Seth asked Madison. He took her arm and drew her out onto the dance floor.

"It's been a long time since I danced with anyone," Madison said.

"Well, we need to change that. You always have been as I remember, and you haven't lost your touch. You're a good dancer," Seth said. "Do you remember our prom?"

"Yes, I do," Madison replied. "I think it was the best day of my life."

When the dance was over, Seth said. "Let me introduce you to the board members. He then led her to meet the members of the company board of directors and their wives. This explained the reason that Seth had invited who he had on his guest list. He had his business in mind.

"Congratulations on your marriage. It's nice that we finally get to meet your secret weapon for taking the spring business by storm," the tall dark man with gray eyes said. "I am Simon Faulk, and this is my wife—Barbara."

"Nice to meet you," Madison said. "I don't know that I'm any kind of secret weapon, but I do try to keep the employees happy and when the employees are happy, they do their best work."

Barbara pulled Madison away from the male board members and soon they were surrounded by other women.

"I like your style," a plump woman of what appeared to be Italian origin said and put her hand out to Madison. "I am Jennifer Lawson. I am the lone woman on the board."

"Well, perhaps in time we can change that," Madison replied. "I think that it's good if we can change some of the way Fisher Springs Inc. operates."

"Though I appreciate your enthusiasm, I think it's best if I warn you to watch yourself, Madison," Jennifer said. "I hate to say this, but the board is still quite patriarchal. "

Barbara Faulk stood between them "Oh, the two of you need to stop all this business talk. Madison is a new bride, and I think she's just beautiful. I love how you kept your dress simple but elegant and fun. My wedding dress was beautiful, but by the end of the reception, I was exhausted from having to carry around all that weight from that ridiculous train!"

The women laughed and for a few minutes, they talked about their weddings and compared them to this one.

After a few minutes, Madison tried to change the subject back to business. "So, Jennifer, would you be interested in looking at an insurance plan that the human resource manager and I had created for the factory workers?"

Jennifer raised her hand motioning for Madison to stop talking. "I would love to see it sometime, but right now, I agree with Barbara. Let's not talk shop. It's time for us to celebrate."

At that same moment, Seth returned to Madison's side and Simon Faulk raised his glass in a toast. "To Ryan and Madison!"

The others in the room joined in the toast as did Ryan and Madison as well.

"I have another surprise for you!" Seth exclaimed.

Seth nodded to two of the factory workers, and the two men moved a curtain. Behind the curtain, on a table was a huge wedding cake with silverware and plates around it.

"When? How?" Madison asked.

"Well, I knew that you wanted to do the wedding yourself, but I knew that you couldn't afford a large cake and..."

"And you invited all these people," Madison replied.

"Exactly. It would be wrong if we at least couldn't offer them some cake," Seth replied. "You don't sound so happy about it."

He looked down at her. His lips pressed together in a line. He looked disappointed that she was not thrilled with his thoughtfulness.

Madison knew that her delight in this cake was important to him, and she never wanted him to see her irritability, but it was obvious, so she said. "It is beautiful."

Ryan and the rest of the kids surrounded the cake. it was time to cut the wedding cake.

The cake was massive and beautiful, and Madison couldn't help feeling irritated. She had planned the wedding so carefully and yet Seth had bought the cake and invited the guests without even telling her that he was doing it. He had smiled down at her when they came up to the cake, she realized that he thought she would be pleased. She tried to pretend that she loved it, but she felt irritated about its existence.

They posed for a photo in front of the cake for the photographer. Seth had arranged for this photographer as well, but Madison knew about this. She was known as one of the best in the area and Madison was amazed that Seth was able to get her on such short notice.

Finally, it came time for them to leave. Each of the guests had been given a small bag of birdseed and Madison and Seth ran between the people on either side of the sidewalk as they pelted them with the birdseed. At the waiting Ferrari, Seth helped Madison into the passenger seat and then went around to the driver's side door and slid into the seat.

"Well, we did it," he said. "He laid his hand on her thigh and then put the car into gear.

"Yes, we did," Madison said but then couldn't think of anything else to say.

They traveled in silence until they arrived at the old house that was to be their new home. Seth pulled into the driveway and drove around to the back. He went around to Madison's side of the car and opened the door.

"Your hand, my lady," he replied. He held out his hand and she placed hers in his. He pulled her to her feet then took her hand and led her to the back door.

"We'd better do this right," he said as they came to the door. He pulled out a key, put it into the lock, and turned it. He then opened the door.

Madison was about to step through the door when he said. "Oh, no you don't."

Before she could respond, she felt her feet lift from the ground and he swung her up into his arms. He then stepped through the threshold into the house. "You did know that I was a traditionalist, didn't you? It would be bad luck if I didn't carry my bride over the threshold."

"It seems to me as if you are a little superstitious," Madison suddenly felt shy. She felt uneasy. They had not discussed the wedding night and she was suddenly self-conscious.

"I need to change out of these wedding clothes," she said. Seth had already loosened his tie and had unbuttoned his wedding shirt.

Madison rushed upstairs and went into the master bedroom. There she saw the box that contained the negligee that the girls at work had given her for a wedding gift. She shook her head. She didn't want to embarrass herself by making Seth think that she wanted something more than a business arrangement for Ryan's benefit. Instead, she took the comfortable flannel pajamas that she normally wore and put them on. She dressed quickly as she heard Seth coming up the stairs. She was hanging up the white dress she had worn when Seth entered the bedroom.

"Wow, that was quick," he then looked at what she was wearing. "That looks comfortable."

Seth removed his jacket and threw it on the bed. He then unzipped his pants.

"I'm hungry," she said. "That cake didn't seem to be enough."

"We could just order in," Seth replied.

"No, that's okay. I'll just look in the fridge."

Down in the kitchen, she opened the refrigerator. She pulled out some cheese and some ham. A loaf of bread and some chips were lying on the counter. This was what the boys had been munching on. Well, another day of this wouldn't hurt. She would go shopping in the morning.

She found paper plates in the cabinet. She looked in the drawers of the counter in front of her and found that it was a silverware drawer. She pulled out a knife and then went to locate condiments in the refrigerator. There was no mayonnaise, mustard, or any type of condiment. She shrugged and closed the refrigerator but left the meat and cheese on the counter. She had finished making her sandwich and was putting chips on her plate when Seth joined her.

Seth had not just changed his clothes but had also taken a shower. His hair was damp. "There's ham and cheese in here. I can make you a ham and cheese sandwich if you want. There isn't any mustard though. We'll need to go to the grocery store tomorrow."

Seth seemed amused. "Sure, I'm guessing you're not the cook that your mother is."

"You're right. I'm not." Madison shrugged. "I guess I never had to cook. Mom was such a good cook, and I have always been doing other things. We'll either need to have her move in soon or eat out a lot more."

"I guess I can't have everything," Seth replied. "Beautiful, check. Smart check Cook-oh well, two out of three ain't bad," Seth sighed and smiled a sly smile that made Madison's heart melt like he used to when they were in high school.

"Oh, you!" Madison exclaimed and slapped him on the shoulder. With that, he grabbed her hand and pulled her to him. He covered her mouth with his. She gave in to the kiss. It was at that moment that she realized that her mother and Ryan were coming through the back door. Seth had kissed her as a performance for Ryan.

Madison stepped back. She felt the color rising into her face. She was embarrassed that she didn't hide how she felt as she reacted to that kiss. She hoped that he wouldn't feel sorry for her if he ever discovered her secret.

"Mom, why is your face red?" Ryan asked.

"Yes," Seth teased. "Why is your face red?"

Madison glared at Seth. He seemed amused.

"I have Ryan's wedding clothes in the car," Diane said and broke the tension in the room "There were also some clothes in the laundry room and some of his sports equipment in the garage. Are you sure that you don't want me to keep him tonight so you can have your privacy?"

No, that's fine, we'll keep him here with us," Madison replied. "This is Ryan's home too, and I'm sure he'd prefer to sleep in his own bed tonight."

"Come on sport," Seth said. "Let's get your things out of Grandma's car, and we'll take them up to your room."

"I'll finish making sandwiches," Madison replied. "There are some chips here too. Would you like a sandwich, Mom?"

"No, thank you," Diane replied. "I'll just go on home."

Seth and Ryan went out to Diane's car to get Ryan's things.

Madison invited her mother to have a sandwich with them.

"No, I think I'll let the three of you have this night together," Diane replied. "I need to get home. When will you be picking up the rest of your things?"

"I'll have Seth drop me off at your house tomorrow," Madison replied. 'That way I can get my car and my things."

Diane nodded and kissed her daughter on the cheek. "Don't worry, my dear. Seth is a good man. Everything will be alright."

Madison wasn't so sure.

Diane passed by Seth and Ryan as she went out the door.

"You all have a good evening."

Seth and Ryan took the items from Diane's car up the stairs.

19

When Seth and Ryan came back downstairs, Madison had sandwiches and chips ready for them on plates.

"Why don't we eat in the family room tonight," Seth said.

"Alright!" Ryan exclaimed.

"Now don't go thinking that it will be every night thing," Madison replied. "Tonight's a special night."

"Yeah!" Ryan exclaimed and took his plate.

Before Seth could answer Madison said. "Don't worry, Ryan, we'll spare you. We won't be "getting mushy" tonight. At least not in front of you."

Ryan then ran into the family room and turned on the twinkling Christmas lights on the tree that they had all put up together. Ryan wanted a tree and Seth made sure they had the decorations and even a live tree even though they wouldn't be living in the house until after the holiday festivities at Diane's house.

Seth took Madison's plate along with his own into the family room. Madison opened the refrigerator door and took out a bottle of juice. She then pulled out two beers that she saw there too. She took two glasses, one for her and one for Seth. She handed the juice to Ryan who was sitting on the floor in front of the television and sat down on the couch.

Seth handed Madison her plate and sat down on the sofa close to her. He smiled at her and again Madison blushed.

"Ewe, Mom, Dad, are you going to get mushy?" Ryan asked as he looked from one to the other.

As Madison ate, she admired the décor of her new family room.

The interior decorator had done a beautiful job on the room and was exactly as Madison had hoped it would be. She had picked out an oriental-type rug in greens and browns that made the room feel inviting. Seth and Madison's books lined the bookshelves that framed the office closet that was presently covered with shutters. Neither Seth nor Madison planned to do any work tonight.

They sat watching a movie on the 82-inch screened television that Seth had insisted they buy until Ryan's normal bedtime. For a few minutes, it felt good for Madison to be a family. This was at least good for Ryan. There couldn't have been a happier boy in the world than Ryan on that day of Seth and Madison's wedding.

"Time for bed, buddy," Madison was relieved that Seth was the one to say it. She had wondered how Ryan would have reacted if she had been the one who told him it was bedtime.

"Ah Dad," Ryan whined.

"Now, son, remember what I said about having friends over," Seth said.

"Yes, Dad," Ryan said and without any fanfare, he went upstairs to get ready for bed.

"How did you do that?" Madison asked.

"I just told him that once the house was completely remodeled, we would let him have friends over."

"I usually have to threaten him to get him to go to bed and you did it just like that."

She snapped her fingers.

"That's the difference between being the "new Dad" and being the "old Mom". Believe me, this honeymoon period between Ryan and I won't last forever. Speaking of honeymoon. Have you thought about where you would like to go?"

Issues at work and all the preparations for the past two months kept her from even thinking about what they would do for a honeymoon. Plus, there was the remodeling of the house that still needed to be completed as well as Madison's next semester's class schedule. Plus, there were still issues at work to work out. It would be a year before they could even think of getting away for a honeymoon.

While Seth was putting Ryan to bed, Madison turned off the lights downstairs and quickly went to the master bedroom, washed the makeup off her face, and brushed her teeth. She then went back into the bedroom and slipped between the cool silk sheets before Seth came in.

"You're going to bed early," Seth replied.

"Yeah, I'm really tired tonight."

"Yes, it has been a long day," Seth agreed. She remained turned away from him as he undressed and slid under the sheets. Her whole body was completely aware that he lay beside her on the bed.

Madison felt as though every fiber in her body wanted nothing more than to have his arm around her. She wanted nothing more than to cuddle up next to him and go to sleep wrapped in his arms, but she fell asleep without allowing herself that pleasure.

Madison awoke suddenly. Someone was breathing beside her and was nuzzling her neck.

"You smell nice," Seth said. Madison felt her body react to Seth's lips on her neck. Her whole body tingled as he nibbled at her ear lobe.

"You don't smell bad yourself," Madison replied and turned over to face him. She was still groggy, and her defenses were not yet up. She allowed herself to be enveloped in his arms and surrendered to his lips on hers.

She felt herself giving in to his embrace. She felt like she was in Heaven. She wanted nothing more than to be in his arms and be his wife. She felt like she was back at the time when she and Seth had been together all those years ago. It was as if nothing had changed. It felt as though things were the same as they were back then.

Things were like they had been back then. She had not used protection nor had Seth and the first time it had resulted in Ryan's conception. It could happen again.

Madison stopped and backed away from him.

"What's wrong?" Seth asked.

"I can't. Not now," Madison replied. "I forgot something important."

"What did you forget?" Seth asked.

"Protection," she said. "I've been so busy that I didn't prepare. . ."

"You've got to be kidding!" Seth exclaimed.

"You don't have any, do you?" she asked.

"No, I thought you would be prepared," he said. "What if we just take our chances? What could be the worst that could happen?"

"I could become pregnant again," Madison replied.

"That doesn't matter, things wouldn't be like they were the last time with Ryan. We're married. We both want more children, right?"

"I can't," Madison got out of the bed on her side to put distance between her and Seth. "Because I can't bring another child into a loveless marriage."

Seth's face turned to stone. His eyes turned dark with anger as Madison had never seen them. Suddenly she saw how much Seth looked like his father. She shuddered.

"I see how it is now," Seth said from between clenched teeth. "Why did you marry me if. . ."

His voice trailed off and he left the room abruptly and went into the bathroom. The shower turned on and a few minutes later Seth returned to the bed with damp skin and wet hair.

'When did you become such a tease," Seth fumed as he crawled back onto his side of the bed. "Why didn't you get yourself to the doctor and get on birth control already? We've had two months from the time we started working on the house to get that taken care of and you just ignored it."

"You know that I was busy, so I didn't have time. You could have just as well gone to the store and picked up a package of condoms, but that didn't happen either! Did it?"

"You didn't have time? Well, I didn't have time either," Seth retorted.

'You had time to invite a bunch of people to our wedding! You had time to purchase a huge cake, but you didn't have time to stop at the drugstore?"

"I did those things because I thought you would like them!"

"Well, you guessed wrong!"

"Right. You don't seem to appreciate anything that I did for you. You didn't care about the wedding or the wedding either, I guess. Loveless marriage you called it. I should have known," he said bitterly and turned away from her and shut off the light.

20

Madison lay in bed trembling. What had just happened? She and Seth had just had their first fight, and it was a big one. The next morning, they continued about their day as though nothing had happened. They maintained a distant politeness for the rest of the weekend. Seth took Ryan and his friend James to the roller rink. Madison stayed home and did some work. She had started updating the procedure manuals for Fisher Springs by incorporating computer usage.

She was afraid she had made a big mistake. She didn't know how long Ryan's bright and bubbly feelings would be enough for Seth and her, but for now, it would have to do. Seth looked as miserable were miserable she felt, but they would stay together for Ryan's sake. She knew that Seth would insist.

After a Chinese carry-out dinner that evening, together as a family they took down the Christmas tree in the living room that they had put up for Ryan's benefit. The tree was the only decoration that they had put up this year.

They could be more festive next year when the whole house was finished. For this year, the tree was all anyone had time to put up. She had her doubts that there would even be one next year.

On Monday morning, Madison and Seth returned to work driving their respective cars. Everyone teased them about not going on a honeymoon. Again, they forced themselves to act as though they were a happy newlywed couple which they were not.

When Madison was walking through the plant to see how well

everyone was doing with the year-end inventory, she heard one of the workers whispering to one of the other workers and she heard her name. She also heard Seth's name. She now knew that they saw that there was no fairytale ending for her and Seth.

To top it off, their work synergy was off. Soon Madison knew that everyone at the factory was aware that Madison and Seth were unhappy newlyweds.

Madison threw herself into her work. She finished the procedural manual she worked on and then looked over the plans that the interior designer had for upgrades for one of the unfinished bedrooms. She took some notes but remained restless.

That afternoon, Seth came out of his office and over to Madison's. He had not been in her office since they returned to work that morning He barely stepped inside the door.

"I just got word that our biggest buyer is considering going with a different company."

"Do you want me to send our best salesman to the company?"

"No, this is too big a contract to leave in the hands of a salesperson. I can't afford to leave this responsibility to anyone else. I need to go myself. The company had been with the company under my father for as long as I can remember. I need to let them know that they are still in good hands under me as they were under my father."

"Better, if you ask me. I guess that means you'll be leaving in the morning."

"No, I am leaving right now. I'll stop by the house to pack my suitcase, and then I'll stop by Ryan's school to let him know that I'll be gone for a few days."

"Do you know when you'll be back?" Madison asked.

"No, I will call to let you know how things went," Seth replied. He sounded so businesslike.

"Alright," Madison said. "I'll let the rest of the staff know that you are gone for a few days."

"I knew I could count on you, Madison," He hesitated as if he were thinking about kissing her, but then shrugged and walked out the door.

As soon as Seth left, Beca, the receptionist, came into Madison's office.

"What is wrong between the two of you? You need to kiss and make up or you're both going to self-destruct,"

"It's personal. It is none of your business," Madison said.

"That's where you're wrong!" the receptionist replied. "Anyone can see that you're in love with each other, but . . ."

Madison's jaw dropped. "Are you saying you think Seth is in love with me?"

"Of course, he is, you dope. Any fool can see that. Why did you marry him if not because you loved him," she asked.

"I... our son Ryan."

"Your son had nothing to do with it. I know that the reason you stuck with this job when Harrison treated you like dirt was not because you needed the money. You could have gone anywhere you wanted to work, and you could have told the old man to put it where the sun doesn't shine, but you didn't. Why? Because I know as well as you do that you wanted to be here if and when Seth inevitably returned."

"I..." Madison hadn't thought about that before but what Beca said was true.

"I rest my case," Beca pursed her lips together as if to emphasize her position.

"But he doesn't love me. He just needs me to. . ."

"You have no idea. Do you?"

Madison shook her head. 'What do you mean?"

"I am surprised that you haven't noticed how he looks at you whenever the two of you are in the same room. It's been that way ever since he came back in town."

Madison thought about what Beca had said. She decided to ask Janice what she thought.

"I don't know what's going on between the two of you either," Janice replied. "You had such a wonderful chemistry before you got married and then after the wedding, but after marriage, you both act like the wedding certificate was your death certificate."

Madison shook her head. How could she have been so wrong? More importantly, would Seth be able to forgive her for all the nasty things she had said to him?

21

~

Madison didn't hear anything from Seth and what issue he faced with the company he visited.

During that time, she kept herself busy. At home, she continued working with the interior designer and the contractor as they now focused on the grand living room and front hallway. When they tore up the carpeting in the entry hall, they found that the wood flooring had been water-damaged so they would need to replace it.

On Tuesday the interior designer called Madison. The cost of repairs and redesign of the house was mounting. The wood floor in the front entryway under the green shag carpet in front of the door was damaged and the floor needed to be replaced. It would be difficult to match modern flooring with the existing flooring.

"What do you suggest?" Madison asked.

"Well, I think that it would be best if you replaced the wood flooring with tile flooring. Let me message you a terracotta tile that I think would be perfect."

"Alright, but I should talk to my husband about it before I make my final decision."

"That's not a problem," I'd be happy to forward the picture to him.

"No, that's alright," Madison replied. "I can forward the photo to him."

The first couple of times she tried to call him she left a message, but when he didn't call back, she figured that if he had any issues about her decisions, she would tell him that for whatever reason they would sell the house, the tiles in the entryway would increase the value of the house almost as much as the curb appeal that Seth had insisted on.

Tuesday night, Madison decided to call Amanda, the realtor, about that to see if what the designer said was true. She said that the advice was sound. At least she could tell Seth that both the designer and the realtor agreed.

On Wednesday morning, Madison called the interior designer that the terracotta would be fine.

"Good choice," said the interior designer, "the entryway is where you make the first impression, so you want to be sure to put your best foot forward. Having tile here will make a big difference."

Since Madison couldn't contact Seth, she also had to make decisions at work in Seth's stead. They were getting orders beyond what they could fill, and she decided to keep some of the staff on specific machines in over-time for Wednesday afternoon. It would mean costing them time and a half, but again Madison could justify the overtime by the fact that the orders would go out on time rather than put the springs on back order into the New Year.

Finally, on New Year's Eve morning, Seth called.

Because she was at work when he called, she kept the conversation business-like.

"Thank God you called," Madison replied. "I wasn't able to get through to you and I had to make some decisions."

"What kind of decisions?" Seth asked.

She told him about the decisions regarding the house and regarding giving some of the workers overtime.

"I'm sure that's fine if the overtime can be justified. I think you did great. It sounds like you have everything under control. Just as I expected you would." He was speaking as she was in an all-business-like tone.

Seth replied. "I have some more good news myself."

"You do?" Madison asked. "So, your meeting went well?"

'Yes, it was dicey at first, but once I sorted out the numbers for them, they were ready to stay with us."

"That's great," Madison decided to broach the subject of their marriage. She felt anxious broaching the subject, but she knew that one of them had to. "When you get back, we need to talk."

"I agree," Seth replied. "I'm coming home tonight and I want to take you and Ryan out to dinner when I get home. Ryan doesn't have anything going tonight, does he?"

"No, he doesn't,' Madison was confused. She didn't know what Seth had planned. She hoped that the two of them would be able to deal with their differences. "He will be happy to know that you are coming home tonight. He has missed you.'

She half expected him to ask her if she missed him too, and she was disappointed when he didn't.

After she got off the phone with Seth, she called her mother and told her that she was going to pick up Ryan who was staying with his grandmother that day while Madison worked.

"You are?" Diane asked. "Why are you getting off work early?"

"Ryan and I are meeting Seth at the restaurant by the country club."

"Does that mean that you have worked things out?" Diane asked.

"Well not exactly," Madison answered. "Not yet, anyway, but it is on the agenda."

"You need to come clean with him and tell him how you feel," Diane replied. "If you don't, you may never know exactly where he stands."

"I think I already know."

"You know what they say about assuming," Diane said.

"Yes, Mother. That's why we need to talk and lay our cards out on the table."

"Finally!" Diane exclaimed. "Isn't that what I've been telling you all along?"

"Yes, Mother

After work, Madison went to pick Ryan up from her mother's house.

"Hi, Mom!" Ryan said as she came in her mother's front door.

"Well, hi, son, what have you been doing all day?"

"Oh, just watching football. I wish Dad was here to watch it with me," he replied.

"Well, guess what! We're going to get all dressed up and meet your father at Reggie's Restaurant.

"Oh, Mom, do I have to get dressed up just to eat dinner?"

"Yes, we're going to Reggie's and they have a dress code. If you don't want to get dressed up for dinner, perhaps I can leave you here with your grandmother."

"You mean I wouldn't be able to go with you to see Dad?" Ryan's eyes grew wide. Madison knew that if he took her up on the offer, it would not only disappoint Ryan but Seth too.

"That's right," Madison replied.

"Okay, I'll do it."

Just then Madison's phone rang. "I wonder who that could be? I don't recognize the number."

Diane and Ryan both were looking at her as she answered the phone. "Hello?"

"Mrs. Fisher?" Madison didn't recognize the voice at the other end of the line either.

"Yes."

"Mrs. Seth Fisher."

"Yes."

"I'm sorry to have to be the one to tell you this, but your husband has been in an automobile accident," the person on the other end of the line said. "They're taking him to the hospital by ambulance."

"What?" Madison's hands began to shake. Her voice choked. She could hardly breathe. "How bad?"

"I can't discuss this over the phone."

"Which hospital?" Madison imagined Seth lying in a hospital bed.

"He's being taken to Springfield Trauma Hospital."

Madison was numb she barely registered what the police officer said. She did hear that he was in the emergency room and that the doctors were with him then.

What's the matter, Mom?" Ryan saw the worry on her face.

"Your dad has been in an accident. I must go to him."

"I'm coming with you, right?"

Madison shook her head. "No, I'm sorry. You'll need to stay here at your grandma Diane's house."

"No, Mom, I want to go with you."

"I'm not staying at grandma's," Ryan screamed. "Please don't make me stay here."

"You've got no choice, "she insisted.

Madison just realized that she had not even asked her mother if she was willing to keep Ryan. "It is alright, isn't it, Mom?"

"Oh, honey, of course, Ryan needs to stay here," Diane replied. "I'll find something for Ryan to sleep in and I'll go by your house tomorrow to get him more clothes."

"Ryan, as soon as I find out anything, I promise that I'll let you know how your dad is doing," Madison said. Ryan was still pouting but was now resigned to the fact he wasn't going to convince Madison to let him go with her.

When Madison arrived at the emergency room, staff, patients, and patient family members rushed in every direction. She went up to the emergency desk.

"I'm looking for a patient," Madison said. "His name is Seth Fisher. He was in an accident. I'm his wife."

The receptionist directed her to a room and a nurse took her there. When Madison arrived at the room, they were just wheeling Seth out of the room he lay unconscious on the emergency room gurney.

She was first greeted by a paramedic. "Can you tell me what happened to my husband? I just heard that my husband Seth Fisher had been hurt."

"Yes, my partner and I were the ones who brought him in. His car was involved in a head-on collision with a drunk driver. The other driver, of course, came through without a scratch. We stabilized your husband at the scene and brought him here to the emergency room. The doctor is with him now."

The paramedic led her to one of the emergency trauma rooms. There Seth lay on an emergency room gurney. A doctor stood over him and was writing in a metal folder. He handed the metal folder to a nurse next to him and that nurse and another one began wheeling the gurney out of the emergency room toward the elevators. The doctor saw Madison.

"Are you Mrs. Fisher?" the doctor asked.

"Yes," she said breathlessly.

He directed Madison into a consultation room.

"Your husband is a very sick man. Will you sign the papers for me to operate? We must get him into surgery as soon as possible."

"Operation? What's wrong?"

"He has a collapsed lung." He then gave the details of the condition.

Yes, I'll sign," Madison replied. The nurse who was with the doctor put a clipboard in front of her and instructed her where to sign as she explained the procedure to Madison. With a shaking hand, Madison signed the pile of documents the nurse put in front of her.

The nurse then directed her out to the main desk of the emergency room to a young girl wearing a green blouse. On her chest was a pin that read "volunteer".

"Candi, can you show Mrs. Fisher here where the operating waiting room is."

"Of course, Barbara," she said.

Candi led Madison through the maze of hospital hallways to the operating area waiting room. It was a large room with several television screens around the room. To one side was a wall filled with vending machines. Chairs, tables, and couches were arranged throughout the room.

Madison took a seat at the back of the room near one of the television sets. There was an old movie on, but she didn't pay much attention to its plot. She sat there for what seemed like forever.

She received a text from her mother asking her what she found out. She called her.

"Hi Honey, what's going on?" Diane asked. "How's Seth?"

"I don't know, Mom," Madison burst out in tears. 'He's in surgery!"

"Oh no, what exactly happened?"

Between sobs, Madison told her about the accident."

"His car?" Diane asked.

"I don't know, Mom," she said. "I guess I'll have to call the police or something."

"There will be time for that later," Diane said. "Are you sure you don't want me to come up there with Ryan?"

"No, Mom, Ryan is better off at home or at least at your home. There's nothing you can do here." Madison's voice broke during the last few words.

"Don't worry. Seth will get through this, and you'll work it all out between you. Just be honest with him when you get the chance, okay."

"Alright," Madison replied. At that moment, the doctor came out into the waiting area.

He held his mask in his hand. "Would you come with me, please, Mrs. Fisher?"

He led her to another consultation room. Not sure what the doctor was going to tell her, she feared the worst.

The doctor patted her on the shoulder.

"You'll be relieved that the surgery went well," the doctor said. "We placed a tube in his chest and his condition is stable. He will require a few days in ICU, but barring additional complications like infection, he should recover without lasting effects. You can see him in the recovery room now if you'd like."

A different nurse led her to the recovery area.

Seth lay still in the recovery room and dressed in a hospital gown. His eyes were closed, and his face was an ashen gray color. He had a black eye, and a bandage covered the right side of his head. He looked as if he were dead. A tube with a bag filled with blood hung from the side of his bed. An oxygen cannula hung around his ears and its prongs hung in his nose. If it weren't for the monitor beeping beside him and his regular breathing, she could have mistaken him for dead.

Tears welled up in Madison's eyes. She pulled up the chair beside his bed and held his hand in hers. His hand was cold, and his whole body was trembling, but he didn't respond to her touch.

"I just want you to know I'm here for you and I love you," Madison said. Holding his hand in hers. She pressed the hand to her lips.

She laid her head down on his chest on the opposite side of Seth's body where the drain was attached. She felt comforted knowing that with every beep of the machine behind him, he was on his way back to her.

Suddenly she felt his free hand move to surround hers.

"You're awake," Madison exclaimed.

"Yes, I'm glad you're here," Seth said. "Can you give me a drink of water? There's a cup here on the table beside the. . ."

"I see it," Madison replied. There was a plastic cup and straw. She picked up the cup and put the straw into his mouth. He took a sip and then motioned for her to take it away.

Seth replied. "I love you too."

"You heard me say that?" Madison asked.

"Why didn't you tell me."

"Why didn't you tell me?"

"I asked you first," Seth laughed and then winced in pain.

"You came here, and you took over my life just like you did when we were in high school. I was making a life for myself before you came. I had dreams. I was raising Ryan. I was getting my education so I could make something of myself. It wasn't perfect, but it was my life, and I was happy, but then you came along. You took over just like you had back then. I was afraid that if I let my guard down you'd leave me again."

"Couldn't you tell I just wanted you to be happy. It seemed like the more I did for you, the more dissatisfied you were."

"You forced your way back into my life. You did things because they were things you wanted. You wanted all those guests at the wedding. You wanted that big wedding cake. You wanted us to live in that big house."

"I thought that was what you wanted."

"Maybe it was, but I couldn't figure that out for myself because you took over. I wanted to do it myself or at least have a say on how things are done. You didn't even ask what I wanted or even if I thought it was okay."

I thought that was what you wanted. I thought I was helping you."

"But you weren't. You don't have to do my thinking for me. You know that I can think for myself."

"Obviously."

"Not so obviously!"

"I guess not. I didn't realize that you were so insecure. I thought you thought the same way that I did."

In a lot of ways we do, but I don't like the way you were taking over my life again. I was afraid you'd leave me again," she replied.

"Just to be fair, I didn't exactly leave you. I was always going to Germany to become an engineer."

"It's because after you left, you married that other woman."

"You were jealous that I married Bianca?"

"Yes."

"I guess I should be flattered, but It was one of the biggest mistakes of my life," Seth took in a jagged breath.

Madison looked up at him. "What do you mean?"

"Do you why that marriage didn't last?" he asked.

"No," She whispered.

"It's because I realized that I was still in love with you."

Now she could barely breathe. Could it be?

Tears sprang to her eyes. "Really?"

Seth squeezed her hand with his left hand, the one with the IV. With his right hand, he touched the dampness on her left cheek. "Oh, baby, don't you know that I love you too? I've always loved you."

"You've never said. You said you needed me, but you never said you loved me."

"Of course, I need you. I need you in so many ways. You're the mother of the best boy in the world. You're my right hand on the job. You're my best friend. You're the one person I want to spend the rest of my life with. I can't imagine life without you."

"It would have made a difference if you said this to me before."

"I'm an idiot," he exclaimed.

"We both are," Madison replied and kissed him on the forehead.

At that moment, the nurse came in and said that they were moving him to his ICU room. Madison was directed to the ICU waiting room where another nurse came to get her when Seth was settled in his room.

While she waited, she called her mother again.

"He's out of surgery," Madison said. "Tell Ryan that his dad was hurt in an automobile accident, but it looks like he'll be okay."

"I will. He will be happy to hear that," Diane replied. "I guess you haven't had a chance to talk about your situation?"

"Matter of fact, we did, and I think everything will be okay between us."

"I'm glad," Diane said. "Have you called Seth's mother?"

"No, I didn't think of it," Madison replied.

"Well, you need to do that. You are Seth's wife so it's your responsibility."

"Yes, Mother, Madison replied.

Madison hung up from the call and then called Seth's mother. It was in the middle of the night there and Mariya had been asleep.

"Madison? Why are you calling me?" Mariya said. "Is something wrong?"

Madison replied. "Seth's been an accident."

An accident," the urgency could be heard in her voice.

"Yes, Seth's car was hit by a drunk driver."

"Is he going to be alright?"

"He's in ICU here, but I believe it is primarily a precaution. The doctor seemed to indicate that he should have a full recovery."

"Oh, thank God," she exclaimed. "Would you like for me to come stateside again?" Mariya said.

"But your business. . ." Madison started.

"Since Christmas is over, the business can take care of itself for a while. I have some good people working with me," Mariya said. "It sounds like Seth is going to be out of commission for a while so if it is okay with you, I'd like to come to help with your business. Plus, I'll get the chance to spend more time with my grandson. I want to make sure that the vultures in his business don't try to take over his business."

"You and me both," Madison replied.

"Then it's settled. I will fly out there as soon as I can get a flight. I can't wait to get to know Ryan better."

Madison laughed. "You and Seth are going to spoil that boy rotten."

"A good boy is like good wine. He can't be spoiled. He'll just get better as he ages," Mariya said.

A few moments after the phone call ended, A nurse called Madison to Seth's ICU room. Again, the monitor was beeping.

"We just gave him some medication for pain, so he will probably be drowsy," the nurse replied.

"Did you get those birth control pills yet?" he asked. His eyes were getting to the point where they seemed to have difficulty focusing.

"No, not yet. I have an appointment with the doctor on Tuesday."

"Would you cancel it?" Seth asked. "Ours is not a loveless marriage after all. I want us to have a little girl just like you."

"We'll wait until your lung is completely healed," she said.

Seth smiled, because of the medication, his eyes were losing their focus.

Epilogue

On the first day of spring, a Friday in March, one of the loading docks at the factory was lined with tables filled with all kinds of food that the company's employees had all brought that morning for a potluck lunch. Over one of the tables was a banner that read: *Happy Retirement, Pete!*

The tables were placed in a large square, and the chairs were arranged so that no employee would be able to miss details of the festivities. Pete sat at the center of one of the tables and was just finishing up his second plate of food.

Seth's empty seat was right of Pete and Madison sat on the right of Seth's seat.

Where's your husband?" Pete asked Madison.

"You'll see," No sooner had Madison spoken the words that Seth wheeled a table that contained a cake that he asked Madison to order several days earlier for the party. The cake with white frosting had words written in red that said, "*Enjoy Your Retirement, Pete.*"

"For me?" Pete asked. "What are the rest of you going to eat?"

Everyone laughed.

Madison put her hand on the baby bump which was just starting to show through her maternity top. A few days earlier she and Seth had discovered that they were going to have another boy, and they had told only Ryan. Even Diane was still left in the dark about her second grandson.

When they told Ryan the evening before, he had been ecstatic about having a brother. Madison mused as she remembered how he and Seth spent the evening talking about how they would teach him various sports.

A lot had happened since Seth's accident. True to her word, two days after Seth's accident Mariya had come to help with the business. She conducted meetings with the sales staff, production managers, and the human resources departments and taught Madison a lot about the business. The business that Mariya ran in Germany was almost a mirror image of the one in the States. Although some of the laws were different in the other countries, Mariya made sure that Madison was well-versed in the business as they applied to US laws.

In the process, Mariya made several changes and made some suggestions for ways that would be more efficient than the ones that Harrison had instilled in the company. Under her watchful eyes, profits in the business were already soaring.

Though Seth wasn't always happy with the arrangement and wanted to get back to work, Mariya made him stay home for a couple of weeks after returning home from the hospital so that he fully recovered. During those two weeks, Seth spent his hours at home looking for a car to replace the Ferrari that had been wrecked. He opted for an SUV instead of another sports car.

When he returned to the office, Mariya spent a week getting him up to speed and then flew back to Germany to return to her own business.

With Seth back at work, he and Madison went back to their routine of working together. Every night that he could, Seth spent with Ryan. It was as though he were making up for the seven years that he had lost. After Ryan went to bed, however, Seth devoted his time to his wife.

Now they were celebrating the retirement of a valuable employee.

Madison looked up at Seth and Seth met her eye to eye. Madison was no longer afraid that the other shoe was going to drop. She now knew that she could trust Seth and not only did Seth have the company's best interests at heart, but she also knew that he had her best interests in his heart as well.

She knew that this wasn't a happy-ever-after story either. She knew that she and Seth would not always see eye to eye, but she knew that they could work through their differences. As co-workers, as parents, and as husband and wife, they would work together.

Cygnet Brown lives in the Missouri Ozarks. She is the author of the historical fiction series *The Locket Saga*. She produced her first book *When God Turned His Head* in 2013.

Other books in The Locket Saga include:

Soldiers Don't Cry, The Locket Saga Continues
Book III of the Locket Saga: A Coward's Solace
Book IV of the Locket Saga: Sailing under the Black Flag
Book V of the Locket Saga: In the Shadow of the Mill Pond
Book VI of the Locket Saga: The Anvil

Nonfiction by Cygnet Brown

Simply Vegetable Gardening
Help from Kelp
Using Diatomaceous Earth Around the House and Yard
Living Today, The Power of Now
Write a Book and Ignite Your Business
The Survival Garden,
Gourmet Weeds co-authored with Kerry Kelley.

Check out her blogs https://authorcygnetbrown.com and https://the-perpetual-homestead-er.com to learn more about Cygnet's current activities.

9 789898 791532 5